MADDIE'S AWAKENING

THE LIFE AND TIMES OF MADDIE RANDALL

MARY ANN BRANTLEY

Proverbs 3:5 Trust in the Lord with all thine heart; and lean not to thine own understanding. 6. In all thy ways acknowledge Him and He shall direct thy paths. (KJV)

This is a work of fiction. Names, characters, and incidents either are products of the author's imagination or are used fictitiously. Any resemblance to actual events or persons, living or dead, is entirely coincidental.

Copyright © Mary Ann Brantley 2015

To Abba

CHAPTER 1

East Tennessee, 1969

Maddie wiped the sweat from her brow, pushed her hair off her forehead with her arm, and mumbled. "He is a sloppy, slapdash of a man, if ever there was one."

She made three neat stacks and one towering pile of the rubble she'd tossed from the watercraft, and stood the garden hoe, leaf rake, and shovel in the corner. The empty motor oil cans, pesticide bottles, newspapers and greasy rags mounded to waist high. The other two piles contained used tires and pine slabs. She would have discarded them along with the rags, bottles, and cans, but her Daddy would want to keep them for one of his do-it-yourself projects.

"There's a storm coming," Belva said, cautioning her daughter from the wobbly back porch of their unfinished, three-bedroom rancher. "You shouldn't go out on the lake today."

"We won't be out long, Momma," Maddie called back from the rickety old boat shed where she had spent the morning cleaning her dad's homemade pontoon boat. Cal had made it last summer when he had one of his I-can-make-it-cheaper-than-I-can-buy-it epiphanies. He had built a wooden raft atop two sealed polystyrene chemical barrels filled with compressed air. The cover was a canvas awning attached to four steel posts he had fabricated on his job at the steel mill. The watercraft was hideous, but it worked.

"Does your daddy know you're planning to take the boat out?"

Maddie knew better than to lie to her mother, but she figured a tiny fib could do no harm. "We discussed it yesterday," Maddie said from beneath the boat trailer while still swiping cobwebs off the wheels.

She and Cal had discussed it last night, but as usual, they didn't agree. When Maddie asked him if she could take her two best friends to the lake for the weekend, he said, "Girls got no business on the lake without a man to look after them."

"You are such a chauvinist," she had muttered under her breath. "I don't need a man looking out for me. I can take care of myself." Now she was determined to do it, or die trying.

Cal had pointed his finger in her face and retorted, "I said no, no is what I meant, and we're done talking about it."

"He said I couldn't take it out for the weekend, Momma. Val, Wynona and I are cruising over to Poor Land Cove for the afternoon. We'll be back before the storm comes."

Maddie backed her mud-brown 1960 Volkswagen Carmen Ghia up to the boat trailer and fastened the trailer to the hitch before going back inside. Changing into a red and white bikini, hidden beneath a baggy shirt and ragged denim shorts, she kissed Belva on the cheek and said, "I love you, Momma." As an afterthought, she grabbed an apple from the bowl on the table then danced out the back door to the music of Credence Clearwater Revival blaring from her transistor radio.

Maddie opened the windows in her mud-mobile and let the wind whip through her long, blonde hair. She maneuvered with finesse through the five miles of switchback curves on the road to Mountainside State Park, all the while ignoring the voice in her head telling her to go back home. She couldn't turn back now. Wynona and Val were already at the dock waiting for her.

At the lake, she backed the boat into the water and lowered the outboard motor. "We're going out for the afternoon, Wynona. I'm sure you don't need all those hair brushes and makeup cases. No one will be there who cares if your hair is in place or your face is painted to perfection." Maddie glanced at Val, who rolled her eyes and shrugged her shoulders.

"I don't care what you say, Maddie. I'm taking it with me. I couldn't bear to be seen in public with no makeup on. You know how it washes away when I'm in the lake. And my hair frizzes with the least bit of moisture." Wynona patted her hair, making sure it was in place.

"Jeez, Wynona," Val said. "I never notice when you have on makeup and when you don't, and your dishwater blonde hair is always frizzy. Besides, you'd be a lot more likeable if you weren't so vain."

Wynona gave Val a distasteful head-to-toe ogle. "And you could benefit from fixing yourself up like a lady. Those spikey black bristles you call hair remind me of a porcupine, and your lips are the same shade as your skin. Looks like you don't have any."

"At least I'm not afraid to be myself. But you—"

"Take me home, Maddie. I refuse to spend the day with this—this—jerk!" Wynona shoved her makeup case back into trunk of the VW and slammed the lid.

"No, Wynona," she said as she looped the tow rope over the dock post. "We are not going back home. We are going to Poor Land Cove."

Wynona huffed and re-rolled the cuff on her cut-off denim shorts, tucked in the tail of her bright yellow tee-shirt, and examined her pink painted toenails and purple flip-flops. Val mimicked her actions by tugging at the bottom of her untucked white polo shirt and smoothing the front of her blue plaid Bermuda shorts. She snickered and pushed Wynona's tote bag full of towels beneath the car with her sneaker covered foot.

Maddie checked that everything was stowed beneath the boat seat, started the outboard motor and steered them westward into open water. No one acknowledged the dark clouds hovering above the tree line to the east.

***

Cal sipped his first cup of coffee as he waited for Belva to prepare his breakfast. It was noon when he got out of bed, three hours before his next shift at the steel mill.

"Good morning, Cal." Belva kissed him on the forehead and refilled his cup, then broke two eggs into the frying pan.

"Is Maddie here?" he asked.

Belva opened the oven door and peeked at the biscuits. "No. She, Val, and Wynona took the pontoon boat to Poor Land Cove today. They wanted to spend their last day of spring break together. She said she talked to you yesterday."

"Oh, she talked to me! I told her, in no uncertain terms, she was not taking the boat out for the weekend." Cal ran his fingers through his hair and exhaled a long, infuriated breath. "She'll answer to me when she gets home."

"They're not staying the entire weekend, they're coming back this afternoon," Belva said, while setting a plate of bacon, eggs, biscuits and jelly on the table. "The weather forecast calls for storms this afternoon. I hope she comes back before the wind gets too strong."

"If she gets out on the water and gets stranded, then I guess she'll have what she deserves. Maybe she'll learn to listen." Cal gulped down his food and mopped his plate with his last bite of bread. "Do you have any more biscuits?"

"No, but I'll make you some toast," she said, and reached for his empty plate.

"Don't bother. After I shower and shave, I'm heading over to the garage to get my tire fixed. I'll go to work when I'm done. Fix me two sandwiches to take with me."

Cal shoved his chair away from the table and went outside. Belva turned to the refrigerator and made lunch for Cal. She prayed for Maddie's safety.

CHAPTER 2

"Hey, Maddie! Toss me the tanning oil." Val was closer to the bottle, so she picked it up and tossed it to Wynona, who sat on the edge of the raft dangling her feet in the water. The bottle of oil made a smacking sound when it hit her on the arm.

"Ouch! You did that on purpose, you pod." Wynona grabbed her soda can and aimed it at Val's face.

"Sorry, Wy, I didn't mean to hit you. I have a crooked aim." Val ducked to keep the can from striking her on the nose. "Seriously, Whiney, I get it. You don't like me, but jeez, give me a little credit. I'm not as mean as you think."

"Oh, yeah, that's right." Wynona folded her hands into prayer position beneath her chin, made an innocence face, and fluttered her eyelids. "You're as sweet as angel pudding."

Maddie, who lay sunning on the opposite end of the raft, pulled the towel off her face and scolded. "Stop it, you two. Can't you get along for one day? It won't kill either one of you to be nice." She pointed to the eastern skyline. "We should head home anyway. Those clouds over there do not look friendly."

"We haven't even been in the water yet, Mads. We've got another hour before the rain comes. Just thirty more minutes. Come on. Let's swim to the shore. Miss Whiney-nona over there needs to cool off."

"I'm not sure if we should." Maddie noted the ever darkening clouds and the increasing wind. "I've never had the boat out in rough water."

"Please, Mads. Just one lap then we'll go."

She hesitated, then agreed. "Well, okay, I guess, but just one." The voice in her head urged her to go home, now.

"Fifteen minutes," she said to herself, trying to quell the urgency pounding in her heart.

"I'll race you!" Maddie challenged Wynona, hoping to rev up her snail's pace.

"You know I'm not a strong swimmer, Maddie, and you always win." Wynona slithered into the water and floated on her back just inches from the raft. "I'd rather take my time and enjoy the water."

When Maddie reached the shore, Val had already climbed up the rocky bank and grabbed a vine draping from an oak tree whose branches hung out over the water.
"Look, Maddie, a grapevine swing. Let's try it."

"We don't have time to play, Val. Come on. Let's go back to the boat."

Val wrapped one leg around the vine. "Okay, you stay where you are, I'll swing out to you." She pushed off with her free leg, locked it around the vine and flew through the air above the water.

"Whee!" Val squealed with delight. The water splashed five feet high when she plopped into the lake beside Maddie. "That was fun. I'm going for it again," she said, already half-way to the bank.

"Get back here, Val. The storm is close. We have to go!"

Maddie swam faster as rain drops formed tiny ripples on the water's surface. When she reached the boat, Wynona was nowhere in sight.

"Wynona! Where are you? Come on, we have to get going!"

Val climbed onto the boat, exhilarated from her swing and swim. "Let's come to this spot next time. We can have a ball swinging on that grapevine. Where's Wynona?"

"I don't know, Val. I've called, but she doesn't answer. Let's cruise around the shoreline. She may have gone ashore for a potty break. She mentioned a stomach ache after we ate lunch."

Val pulled in the anchor while Maddie stowed their belongings. They toured around the cove, shouting louder and louder.

"Wynona-nona-ona-ona". Her name echoed across the way.

"Where is she, Val?" Maddie's voice trembled. Raindrops pounded against the water and lightning streaked across the eastern sky. Strong wind gusts rocked the boat from side to side, so hard they had to hold on to the steel posts to keep from being hurled overboard. The rickety raft creaked and groaned under the strain.

"There!" Val pointed to a dead tree floating at the water's edge. "Is that Wynona's tee shirt? There's something yellow stuck in the brush. Take us closer to the shore." Maddie struggled against the wind and waves to navigate the boat as near to the bank as possible without getting the outboard tangled in the tree branches.

"Try to grab it with the oar."

Val reached out with the paddle as far as she could stretch while holding to the steel awning post. Waves forced the boat backward each time they came close enough to hook the shirt. One final try, and she pulled the yellow fabric onto the boat.

"Yep, that's Wynona's shirt, but where is Wynona? She shivered and fought back tears. "What are we going to do?"

***

Belva paced the floor, shuddering with every clap of thunder. The storm rolled in fast and rough. Rain beat against the windows, and each lightning bolt flashed closer and closer to the house. The thicket of pine trees in the back yard swayed in the heavy winds, clapping and banging together like bongos drumming an omen.

"Where is Maddie?" Her fingers trembled against the rotary dial. She mis-dialed twice before reaching the garage.

"Daniel, is Cal there? He said he was coming by there this afternoon."

"No. He was here earlier, but he left half an hour ago. You sound upset, Belva. Is everything all right?"

Belva shook her head as if he were standing beside her. "No. Maddie, Val and Wynona took the old pontoon boat Cal pieced together from junk parts to Poor Land Cove this morning. They should be back by now, and I'm worried sick. I can't find Cal. What should I do?"

"Don't panic, Belva. My friend, Tim Rogers, is a park ranger. I'll call him and ask him to check on the girls. I'll get back to you in a few minutes and tell you what he says."

"Okay." She inhaled and blew out a long, deep breath. "Thank you, Daniel."

Daniel tapped his thumb against the phone hook and waited for a dial tone. "Tim, this is Daniel Hershel. How bad is the storm over there?"

"It's rough, Daniel. I sure hope everyone out on the water was wise enough to get in before this weather hit."

"I need a favor, Tim. Cal Randall's youngest daughter and two other girls were out in Poor Land Cove this morning on a homemade pontoon boat. They haven't come back in yet, and Mrs. Randall is worried. Can you send a patrol boat out to check on them?"

"Sure will. I'll check out the parking lot first though, to make sure they haven't already come and gone. What were they driving?"

"A brown Volkswagen Carmen Ghia."

Daniel heard a squawk when Tim keyed the mike on his radio. He tapped his pencil on the desk and counted the seconds.

"I need a ten-twenty on all rangers near dock parking."

"Ten-four, Tim. This is Sam. I'm patrolling the dock area now, over."

"Is there a brown VW Ghia with a boat trailer parked over there, Sam?"

"Affirmative on the Ghia, over."

"Ten-four, Sam. Over and out."

He keyed the mike again. "Attention please, we have a possible emergency in Poor Land Cove. Prepare for water rescue." Tim alerted the rangers, then returned to his phone conversation.

"I'm sending a crew out there now, Daniel."

"Thank you, Tim." Daniel relaxed his shoulders and laid his pencil down. "I'll tell Mrs. Randall. Keep us posted."

Belva grabbed the phone on the first ring. "Hello?"

"Belva, Ranger Rogers is organizing a rescue team to check out Poor Land Cove. If those girls are out there, they will find them. I'll let you know when I hear from him."

"Thank you so much, Daniel. God bless you." She hung up the phone, sat on the sofa with her head in her hands, and cried.

***

"Did you hear that, Val?" Maddie yelled, trying to cast her voice above the noise of the wind and rain.

"Hear what?" Val shouted back. "I can't hear anything but the noise from this horrid storm."

"Someone called my name, and it sounded like he was right beside—."

"You're panicking, Mads. Get a grip." Val made tiny circles with her finger while pointing toward her ear. "Don't get loopy on me."

"No, Val. It was so distinct." Maddie turned in a circle, expecting to see someone nearby.

"Whatever you're doing, Maddie, it's not funny. We need to get off this boat until the storm breaks, then we have to get help. Something terrible has happened to Wynona, I just know it."

"I sure hope not," she said, still probing the shoreline. "Let's find shelter."

Rain stung their skin and thunder echoed through the cove. Maddie shut down the outboard motor and lifted it out of the water and onto the raft, then grabbed the other oar. With great effort, she and Val forced the boat to the bank. Together they secured the tie-down ropes around the tree. Val grabbed the flapping, ragged canvas cover and tried to hold it steady while Maddie picked at the knots in the ropes. When it loosed from one post, a strong wind grabbed it and ripped it in two. They wrangled the torn-off strip into the water and dragged it to land, ripping and tearing it even more as it entangled itself in the branches of the fallen tree. Once ashore they huddled under the tarp, closed their eyes, and prayed the storm would soon pass.

CHAPTER 3

Wynona grabbed her shirt off the pontoon boat and swam fast and hard toward the shoreline, mumbling to herself. "How can this be happening? We didn't even bring toilet paper. What bungling idiots! Who goes out on a boat for an entire day and doesn't remember to bring necessities? I'll just have to use my favorite tee shirt. Lord, I hate to do that."

"What the. . .? Oh my, Lord. Have mercy! Let go of my shirt you, you, stupid tree branch. I need that." The tee shirt stuck tight to the dead cedar. "Oooh, never mind. Nature won't wait." She forged through the water, flailing her arms and legs with all her strength. Up the bank and off to the woods Wynona bolted through a meadow. Suddenly, she pitched forward and landed face down in the mud. Ker flop! Her ankle throbbed. Her foot had been swallowed up in a hole the size of a gallon-sized bucket, covered over by wind-flattened, saturated wildflowers. Feeling like a mud wrestler who had just lost to the competition, she rolled over, pulling her knee to her chest and . . .

"Oh, no! Not now!" Nature's call waited no longer. The rain poured, the wind gusted, and

Wynona cried. Scared and dismayed, she shuddered and shivered while rain drops pummeled her body, chilling her through and through.

She tried to stand, but her ankle---swollen to twice its normal size---ached and throbbed. Pain sliced through her leg all the way to her hip. A lightning bolt struck a nearby cedar tree, splitting it in two. On the verge of an anxiety attack, she chanted, "I will not panic. I will not panic. I will not panic. God, Oh God, please, don't let me die out here with nothing on but my stinky bikini. How embarrassing, even if I am dead." She yelled and yelled for help, but the storm drowned her calls.

Wynona scooted toward an opening in the landscape where a giant, flat rock hung out over the ridgeline, creating a ledge.

***

The rangers and lifeguards climbed into a rescue boat and thrashed through the blinding rain and treacherous waters. Urgency drove them forward through progress that seemed destined to delay. When they reached Poor Land Cove, the thunder and lightning had slowed to light rain.

"Look for a raft, or parts of one," Tim instructed. "The pontoon boat is a rough-and-ready. It might have split apart during the storm."

Tim's voice bellowed through the megaphone while even pairs of roving eyes searched the water and the shoreline for signs of hope.

***

"Val, shh." Maddie laid her finger across her lips.

"Are you hearing voices again?" Val asked, while crawling out from beneath the canvas.

"Yes, I am, and it's coming from across the cove."

Both girls scrambled down the embankment to the boat. To their surprise, it was still afloat.

"Over here!" Val shouted, waving Wynona's yellow tee shirt high in the air. "Help! We're over here!"

"Thank you, God," Maddie whispered under her breath. "I hope they can find Wynona."

"Are you girls hurt?" Tim asked, as he eased the smaller boat closer to the pontoon.

"We're fine," Val and Maddie said. Their voices chimed together. "But you have to find Wynona."

Two rangers hoisted the girls onto the boat and wrapped blankets around their drenched bodies. "How long has she been missing?" Tim asked.

"Since right before the storm started. Val and I swam over to that grapevine hanging out over the water." Maddie motioned toward the oak tree. "Wynona is not comfortable in deep water, so we left her by the pontoon. We were away from the boat for less than ten minutes. When we came back, she was gone. Please, please, please, you have to find her."

"Okay, ladies, the rangers will tow your raft back to the dock and get you dried out. We'll search for your friend."

"Can't we stay and help you search for her?" Maddie asked.

"No. You two go home and let us search. We'll find her sooner if we don't have to look out for your safety. We'll radio back and keep you updated." Tim urged the girls on, eager to get the search moving.

***

Belva ran out to meet Maddie and Val. "Thank God you two are okay. Come inside and change into dry clothes while I make you something warm to drink."

"Thank you, Mrs. Randall, but the rangers are waiting to take me home. I called my parents from the ranger station, but they won't believe I'm okay until they see it for themselves."

Maddie had never shared her faith with her friends, but with Wynona missing and maybe . . . No. She wouldn't allow her mind to go there. Wynona is fine.

Belva wrapped her arms around her daughter's shoulders and walked her into the kitchen for hot tea and cookies.

As Maddie sat at the tiny kitchen table, still wrapped in the ranger's blanket she glanced around at the tiny kitchen, grateful to be inside and safe. She had always thought the kitchen ugly and inadequate, with its mismatched appliances and partially plumbed ceramic sink supported by a homemade box-type cabinet with no doors. Today, though still ugly, the kitchen was a refuge.

"I should have listened to Cal and not taken the boat out," Maddie said, as Belva placed a steamy cup of hot tea on the table in front of her. "If I had, Wynona would be safe. And I shouldn't have lied to you. Cal and I talked about the boat, but I led you to believe he said I could take it out for the day. He didn't. I'm sorry, Momma."

"We'll talk later. I'm happy you're safe." Belva took Maddie's hands in hers and tugged her to her feet. "Let's pray for Wynona." They kneeled together on the cracked linoleum floor and prayed for God to help the rangers find Wynona.

Maddie finished her tea and cookies and went to her room. Exhausted and terrified, she curled up on the bed and fell asleep, clutching the pajama-clad doll that had been her favorite when she was a child.

"Maddie?"

She awoke, startled.

"Did they find Wynona?" She asked as she scanned the room.

Maddie ran tired fingers through her damp hair and stared at her face in the mirror. Her nose was sunburned, her eyes red-streaked and puffy. "I must have been dreaming," she said to herself. She whispered a prayer.

"God, if you're there, please show the rescue party where to find Wynona. This is my fault. I didn't listen to Cal, and I lied to Momma. How can I fix this, Lord?"

"Trust me."

I am not dreaming. I'm wide awake, and I heard that loud and clear. "Am I crazy?" she asked out loud.

"No, Maddie. Have you forgotten me? I talk to you often, but you pay no attention."

"What? Huh?" Maddie stammered, perplexed that someone who wasn't there answered her.

"I tried to warn you, but you ignored me."

"When? How did you try to warn me?" Maddie talked low, hoping Belva didn't hear. She couldn't decide whether to run, or stay and keep talking.

"In the car before you got to the boat dock. I told you to go back, and I warned you again before you went swimming. Didn't I tell you to go home?"

"You're the voice in my head? That was you? You're making me insane."

"I've waited eight years for you to acknowledge me—."

"Eight years ago, I was nine years old. Why would you say . . . ? Wait a minute." Maddie's heart burned within her as the Holy Spirit carried her back to Macedonia Baptist Church, 1961.

Maddie sat on the pew behind the wood-burning stove in the sanctuary. Old preacher Wilson paced back and forth, back and forth, his Bible in his hand, preaching from his soul. "Ye must be born again." Her heart pounded, and a yearning deep within her heart bade her to come and be saved. She rushed from her seat to the altar and asked Jesus to please save her from that awful place the preacher called hell. The fear lifted, and peace flowed into her heart.

The vision came and went. Maddie stood in her bedroom, joyful tears streaming down her face.

"Oh, my dear Lord, I am so sorry." She fell to her knees and buried her face in her hands. "I've ignored you and taken you for granted. Can you ever forgive me?"

"Yes, I forgive you, and I will be your Abba." The tender, compassionate voice soothed her body and soul.

She raised her head and looked upward. "Why do you want me to call you Abba? Isn't your name Jesus?"

"I love you, Maddie. I call my Father Abba because I love Him, and He loves me. He is my daddy. Do you love me, Maddie?"

"I do, and I'm happy to call you Abba. Cal has never loved me the way you do."

"I will always love you, Maddie, and I want to guide you into the life I have planned for you. Will you follow me?"

"I want to, Abba."

***

"Tim Rogers is on the phone for you, Maddie. He has news."

She rose from her knees, wiped away the tears, and went into the living room. Belva handed her the phone. "Hello?"

"Hello, Maddie. We've dragged the lake at the cove and found nothing. I realize you've had a tough day, but will you come back over here and show me the exact spot where you found the yellow tee shirt?"

"I'll do anything to help find Wynona. Give me twenty minutes."

Maddie hung up the phone and turned to Belva. "Ranger Rogers wants me to go back to the cove with him, Momma. I'll be back as soon as I can."

She unhitched the pontoon boat from her Carmen Ghia and pulled away. She couldn't forget that voice.

At the ranger station, Tim organized a search plan. "We'll search in three-member teams and cover the grid, overlapping each sector. There's less than three hours before nightfall, so we need to cover as much ground as possible. Everybody load up your gear and head out. I'll be along whenever Miss Randall gets here."

***

"Miss Randall, are you ready?" Tim asked.

"Ready." Maddie followed him to the dock where they boarded the boat and headed west.

Tim's cabin cruiser bumped against the rippling breakers. Maddie prayed to Abba as they tore across the water.

"Abba, I am so scared for Wynona. Where did she go? Please help us find her. You are the one who knows where she is. Please keep her safe. Please, Abba, please." She picked at her fingernails and bit her bottom lip, wishing Tim Rogers would go faster.

"The overhang," A now-familiar voice whispered.

She looked upward, wishing she could see Him. What did He mean? Was he trying to tell her where Wynona is?

"Tim, is there a ledge or an overhang somewhere near Poor Land Cove?" Maddie asked.

"Yes, a mile from where we found you. Why do you ask?"

"Could Wynona have made it that far in the storm?"

"I guess it's possible, but a mile in a heavy storm is a stretch. I don't—."

"Can we look there first? I can't shake the feeling she might be there."

Tim smiled and nodded. "We have to start somewhere, might as well be there. Or, better yet, I'll radio ahead and send the search team out there right now." The radio spewed and squawked when he took the microphone off the hook.

"Sam, this is Tim. What's your ten-twenty? Over."

"We're entering the cove, Tim, over."

"Head out toward Flat Rock Ledge and start your search. Let me know when you get there, over."

"Ten-four, Tim. We're on it."

The boat lurched against the wake and churned Maddie's already queasy stomach. The stench of lake water and boat motor exhaust mingled with dread, and regret made her nauseous, but the need to find Wynona spurred her to stay strong.

At the cove, Sam's crew packed first aid supplies, and water into their backpacks and headed out toward the ledge. Ten minutes into the search, Sam radioed back to Tim. "I've found her."

Wynona's body lay curled in fetal position, soaked and muddy, a few hundred yards from Flat Rock Ledge. Her swollen ankle had turned blue, with red streaks shooting up her leg.

"What's her condition?" Tim asked. Static sounded through the radio.

"Sam checked her pulse. She's still alive, but her pulse is weak and she's burning up with fever. Looks like her ankle may be broken. Have an ambulance ready when we get back, over and out."

"Thank God!" Tears poured from Maddie's eyes and her whole body shook, releasing the stress that had kept her tense since Wynona first went missing.

"I have to ask." Tim raised his eyebrows and gave Maddie an inquisitive smile. "Why Flat Rock Ledge?"

Maddie smiled and said, "You won't believe it, but I'll tell you anyway: God told me."

Tim nodded. "You sure are something, Maddie Randall."

***

Sam broke open the emergency ammonia stick and waved it under Wynona's nose. She coughed and sputtered.

"Wynona, can you hear me? We're here to help you. Can you move your leg?"

She shrieked when she tried to move, then blacked out again.

"Stay with me, Wynona." He waved the ammonia stick under her nose a second time then spread a blanket on the ground. "We have to get you off this wet ground, Wynona. We'll be as gentle as we can. Try not to move." The lifeguards lifted her onto the blanket and carried her to drier ground beneath the overhang.

Chapter 4

"Let us sign your cast, Wy." Val grinned and whipped out her fluorescent orange Sharpie.

"Don't you dare write on my cast with that obnoxious orange ink." Wynona tried to slap her away.

"Lighten up, Whiney. Are you afraid if you smile you might break your face too?" Val teased.

"Letting people turn your cast into a work of art is the fun part of having broken bones." Maddie laughed at Wynona's defiant smirk. "If you could see the look on your face your head would shrink into your turtleneck from terror. Val's right. Lighten up."

"Well, if you had been through what I've been through you wouldn't laugh either. How do you imagine it feels to be carried out of the wilderness by four handsome men, wearing nothing but your muddy, stinky, potty-soiled bikini? I am so embarrassed and ashamed. I had a crush on the cute blonde lifeguard, and now if he looks at me, I'll know he's remembering you-know-what. My life is ruined!"

Val roared with laughter and Wynona's temper boiled. She threw her pillow at Val and toppled off the sofa. They laughed even harder. "Get out, you two empty pods. I hate you!"

"You know you love us." Val made a kissy-face and fluttered her eyelashes. "You might still be out there if Maddie hadn't had her *close encounter*." Val taunted Maddie with a ghostly *whoooo*.

"Whoa, Val." Maddie leveled her shoulders and jerked her hands to her hips. "Don't make fun of me."

"I'm sorry, Mads. It's creepy how you hear voices and such."

"God is the one who speaks to me, and He is not creepy, Val." Maddie lowered her hands to her side. Her voice remained snappish.

Val's face reddened, and she twisted her mouth. "Oops! Sorry."

"Will you let us sign your cast, please?" Maddie shifted her focus. "We promise to be nice. Don't we, Val?"

"Sure, I guess, but what fun is that?"

Wynona gave in. "Okay, but no fluorescent ink. This cast is ugly enough without you making it glow-in-the-dark tacky."

Careful to stay beyond Wynona's reach, Val uncapped her Sharpie and drew a large orange outhouse on the front of her cast.

***

Weekends were the only days when Cal spent time at home. Maddie hated it when he hung around the house. "He lives to make me suffer," she said to Belva, while watching Saturday morning cartoons and nibbling on a bowl full of Cheerios. "He's always picking at me. *Your dress is too short, your slacks are too tight, your blouse is too low cut.* And he looks at me with those stormy eyes. I can't tell if he's sizing me up for the kill, or if he's having thoughts a daddy should never have about his daughter."

"He's never tried to touch you in an unacceptable way, has he?" Belva frowned and observed her daughter's response.

Maddie cringed, "No, but he tried to peek into my bedroom one night when I was dressing. I despise the way he looks at me."

"Men are vulnerable where women are concerned." She tacked-off the thread on the back of the button she'd been sewing on one of Cal's work shirts.

"Don't defend him, Momma. If he loved me, he wouldn't leer at me. When will he be home from Uncle Josh's?"

Belva pushed her needle into her pin cushion and put the spool of thread back into her sewing box, then went to the bedroom and came back with the ironing board. "Around eleven o'clock this morning. He said he wanted to talk to you."

"I guess he wants to brow-beat me over the boat incident. I'm going to my room. If he wants me, he can come and get me."

The entrance to Maddie's room was a door-sized opening with no trim. A striped blue curtain hung over it for privacy. Sky blue paint covered the unfinished sheetrock, but did little to improve the looks. Nail heads showed through the paint every few inches apart like grayish-brown polka dots on the wall. Her white chenille bedspread and curtains distracted the eye and gave the room a cozy feel, but nothing could disguise the cracked mirror hanging above the crude dressing table made from rough pine two-by-fours and a piece of scrap plywood. Her room was far from elegant, but it was her refuge.

Maddie grabbed her Bible and threw herself across the bed to read. "I haven't read this since we moved from Granny Nettie's place."

She opened her Bible to the book of Psalms. It had been her favorite when she was younger because it had short chapters. If she read ten chapters a week her Sunday school teacher gave her a colored star to put in her Bible. She turned to the back pages of the Bible and rubbed her fingers across multicolored stars pasted in rows. "I miss those days."

"Read my book on love, Maddie."

Abba's bidding burned in her heart until she went to the bookshelf and got the concordance. She flipped through the pages until she found the word *love*. "Here, this must be it. Love defined."

I Corinthians 13(New KJV)

13: 4 Love suffers long and is kind; love does not envy; love does not parade itself, is not puffed up; 5 does not behave rudely, does not seek its own, is not provoked, thinks no evil; 6 does not rejoice in iniquity, but rejoices in the truth; 7 bears all things, believes all things, hopes all things, endures all things. 8 Love never fails.

"Wow!" Maddie said aloud. "Real love requires a lot from a person." She had no patience or tolerance for Cal, and every time he punished her, she puffed up and pouted. And, oh my, the evil thoughts she sometimes had toward him. She wanted to hurt him whenever he told her to shut up and intimidated her with his authoritative demands. "But," she thought, "he doesn't love me either. It's not my fault I'm a girl and not the precious son he wanted." She shoved the guilt gnawing at her conscience into the pages of her Bible and closed it with a slap.

***

The front door opened and closed with a thud. "Maddie, come in here. You and I have something to settle," Cal said, banging on the wall next to Maddie's bedroom door.

"I'm coming." Maddie trembled and swallowed the lump in her throat, then went to meet her fate.

"Sit." Cal issued the order from his chair where he reclined, gazing at her through fiery eyes. "Don't you have something to tell me, young lady?"

She bit back the tears to hide her dread. "I will get the boat canvas fixed. I saved fifty dollars from my babysitting money. If it's not enough, I'll get a job."

"Yes, you will fix it, but when will you fix your insolence, and mind what I say?" Maddie stared down at the floor and counted the joints between the hardwood strips.

"Look at me when I'm talking to you! It's too late to be sorry, and you well deserve to be ashamed. You almost got your friend killed, girl!" He twisted in his seat and leaned toward her with his hand raised. Glad she was beyond his reach, Maddie held her breath and hoped he didn't get up. She slipped into her protective shell the way she often did when he yelled at her, but not before the tears came flooding out.

"Stop that sniffling. You're just like your mother. I can't talk to either of you without you blubbering all over me." He mimicked a sniffle and rubbed his eyes with his fist.

"I'm sorry, Cal," Maddie whispered, intimidated and shamed by his mocking.

"You're 'sorry, Cal'?" He pounded his fist against the arm of his recliner. "Who are you talking to, young lady? And speak up so I can hear you!"

"I'm sor—sorry, Daddy." She snubbed and choked on the words.

"Go to your room, clean up your face, then get back in here. I want you on that couch until you have learned how to behave. We will talk about what you owe me later."

Abba expects me to love him? How could He ask me to do the impossible? Why didn't He ask me to fly up to heaven on a magic carpet?

Maddie cleaned her face in front of her mirror and made an obscene gesture toward the wall. She huffed back into the living room and plopped onto the sofa, setting Cal off again.

"Go back out and come in again, and do it right this time!" He added fuel to her flame. She bit her tongue to avoid lashing back, ambled out of the room, came back in without looking at him, and sat on the beige imitation-leather sofa, her legs crossed at the knee. His eyes beamed at her exposed thigh, then he tossed her the shirt Belva had left on the end table. "Cover yourself and don't let me see you in that short skirt again!"

She sat there under the burn of his gaze, trying not to wrinkle the shirt Belva had ironed. When he closed his eyes and dozed off, she slipped back to her room and added another entry to her ever-growing account of resentments.

Sunday morning came with sunshine, blue skies, and mockingbirds singing in the dogwood tree outside Maddie's bedroom window. The aroma of bacon and fresh brewed coffee wafted through the hallway, teasing her appetite. She heard Cal in the kitchen teasing Belva about the wiggle in her walk.

"Thank you, Lord," Maddie breathed simple praise to Abba. "At least he's in a good mood this morning."

Maddie slipped her gray sweats over her baby doll pajamas. She flipped her hair forward and did a quick head-to-knee bow and tossed her head from side to side like a lion shaking his mane.

"Good morning, Maddie." Belva greeted her with a ferocious hug and an encouraging smile. "I made your favorite Sunday breakfast. Pancakes and bacon, with Mrs. B's maple syrup."

Maddie poured herself a cup of coffee without speaking to Cal. "Thanks, that sounds scrumptious, Momma. If I go to church this morning, will you go with me?"

"We haven't been to church in a long time. If you'll help me clean up the dishes so I have time to get ready, I'd love to go. Will you go too, Cal?"

Without answering, he looked at Maddie and laughed. "Did you sleep with your head under the pillow?" He teased her the way he always did after having humiliated her into submission, acting as if it had never happened.

Maddie did not want to ruin his mood, so she said, "Uh-huh. I had a fight with my covers last night, and the covers won." She crammed her mouth full of food so she wouldn't have to talk to him again.

Cal left the kitchen and went to the living room to sit in his favorite chair and read the Sunday edition of the *Knoxville News Sentinel*. He read the funnies first and laughed out loud, without sharing the humor.

"Which church are you going to, Sweetie?" Belva asked while they cleared the table.

"I've been remembering when we used to go to church at Macedonia. I want to go there today if that's okay with you." Maddie looked toward Belva for approval.

"That's wonderful, Maddie. Let's hurry and finish so we can get started. I haven't been there since Aunt Ruby quit going two years ago, and I'm looking forward to seeing old friends. I'll be ready in twenty minutes."

The church at Macedonia had changed from the way Maddie remembered it. An electric heat and air system replaced the old wood-burning stove and window-mounted air conditioners. Merlot-colored carpeting covered the floor. Stained glass panes in the window above the pulpit caught the sun and cast rainbow-like rays across the altar, giving the sanctuary a heavenly aura. They had even updated the pews with plush padding.

"Isn't this lovely, Maddie?" Belva's widened eyes glimmered with admiration.

"It sure has changed since we came here years ago," Maddie said. "I hope they haven't modernized the way they worship. I can't imagine any worship being better than what we used to do. The old-fashioned preaching sure got my attention."

They sat in the third pew from the altar. The pianist played the traditional rendition of "Amazing Grace" while several people moved to the front to join the choir. Mr. Kimball was still the song leader, but he looked much older than the last time Maddie saw him. "Turn to page 410, and everybody stand and sing praises to Jesus."

Everyone in the congregation sang. Maddie could not contain the tears when the first hymn resonated throughout the sanctuary. Joy surged through her soul as she sang along. "Near the cross, a trembling soul, love and mercy found me. There the bright and morning star sheds its beams around me."

"You must love us so very much. Thank you, Abba," she worshiped.

After the singing, the elders gathered on the altar. They knelt together, elbow to elbow, and uttered sincere and honest prayers. Maddie, listening to the hum of intermingled, humbled voices sending petitions to God, bowed her head and repented for the years she had wasted. Abba came to her in His Holy Spirit and refreshed her soul.

The worship hadn't changed. The preacher still preached and expounded God's Word so plain a child could understand it, and the people still radiated a warm and inviting spirit. That little church was an embodiment of truth and the love described in I Corinthians 13.

"Momma, does God ever talk to you?" Maddie asked on the drive back home.

"Yes, Maddie, but not the way we talk. He speaks in my heart with a still small voice." Belva studied her daughter's face.

"He talks to me that way too, but since the storm he's been speaking in a real voice. No one else hears it, but I sure do. Is that normal?" Maddie glanced at Belva from the corner of her eye.

"If He is speaking to you in a louder voice, then He must have something special in mind for you. You are blessed to have such communication with Him." She patted Maddie on the shoulder.

Maddie shrugged. "Maybe. He asked me to call Him Abba. It means daddy. I told Him Cal never loved me that way, and He told me to read His love chapter. He wants me to love Cal, Momma. How do I do that when he hates me?"

Belva's face wrinkled in thought. "Cal loves you, Madd—."

"Well, he sure has a strange way of showing it." Maddie's face hardened. "God says love is kind, and Cal is not kind. He's mean." She clenched her teeth, pushed the small of her back into the seat, locked her elbows, and gripped the steering wheel until her knuckles turned white.

"Maddie— honey, this bitterness and hate you have for Cal will destroy you if you don't let it go. It doesn't hurt Cal, it hurts you."

Maddie loosened her grip on the wheel and relaxed into her seat, letting Belva's wisdom sink in. "I never thought about it that way, Momma."

Chapter 5

Monday morning arrived long before Wynona was ready to go back to school. Oh, how she dreaded hobbling through the school hallways on crutches, wearing a cast desecrated by a humongous, fluorescent orange outhouse. The other students would tease her with potty jokes for the rest of the school term, thanks to Val.

"Hey, Wynona, I brought you this toilet paper in case you had to go somewhere in a hurry." Jimmy Jones, the class comedian, pounced on the opportunity the instant he saw her. He pitched a roll of tissue toward her and she batted it back with her crutch.

"Why don't you hang on to that toilet paper, Jimmy? You'll need it when I come over there and beat the stuffing out of your puff-ball-for-a-head." Wynona hobbled to her usual stool at the lab table while the rest of the students giggled. One after another the jokes continued, each one more humiliating than the last, until her temper exploded. She flung her crutch across the room at Jimmy. The crutch slapped against the floor louder than a clap of thunder and landed at the science teacher's feet as he came through the lab door. Mr. Dawson stepped on the crutch at just the right spot. It flipped up on its handle and smacked him square between the eyes. The blow knocked him backwards against the wall where he slumped to the floor, as limp as a wet dishrag. The room went silent except for Wynona's and Jimmy's pounding heartbeats.

Twenty minutes later, paramedics fastened motionless Mr. Dawson to a gurney and wheeled him down the hall to a waiting ambulance. Jimmy stood speechless and popeyed, glaring at Wynona's pale face. Neither spoke nor moved until the screaming emergency sirens faded into the distance.

Wynona broke into a full-blown panic attack–legs trembling, heart pounding, head swirling, and unable to breathe. "Someone call the nurse!" Val shouted. She ran to Wynona and caught her just before she hit the floor.

Miss Thomas, the school nurse, scurried through the door and ran to Jimmy who was still unmoved from his wide-eyed glare stance.

"Not him!" the class roared in unison. "Wynona! She fainted."

"This guy needs help too. I believe he's in shock. What happened in this room? First, an ambulance hauls Mr. Dawson out on a gurney, and now this." She probed for information while poking through her nurse's bag for ammonia to bring Wynona around. "Someone go to the little guy over there and prop his feet above his head. I'll get to him in a moment." The nurse waved her arms and swished the crowd away as though she were shooing flies out of the kitchen. "Everybody move back and give her some air."

Wynona roused to consciousness, then hyperventilated again. "Get me a paper bag." She gasped, sucking in quick, shallow breaths.

Val grabbed a large manila envelope from Mr. Dawson's desk and dumped the contents. She handed it to Wynona, who stuffed her face into it. Minutes later, her breathing returned to normal, but not her demeanor. "I've killed Mr. Dawson, and I'm going to prison! I wish I had died in the storm!"

***

Maddie ran from the library to the science lab as soon as she heard the news. "What happened?"

"I killed Mr. Dawson, Maddie. When I threw my crutch at Jimmy Jones to stop him from pestering me, Mr. Dawson stepped on it and it smacked him in the head. He's dead. Plus, Jimmy is in the nurse's office, traumatized." Her eyes grew large. She breathed harder and reached for the manila envelope again.

Maddie waited for Wynona to control her breathing, then asked, "Did the paramedics put a sheet over Mr. Dawson's head when they wheeled him out?"

"No, they strapped him to a rolling cot and put him in an ambulance." Wynona whined a pitiful whimper and stuffed her nose back into the envelope.

"Then he's not dead. They always cover a dead person's face, and if he died the police would be here asking questions."

"Are you sure, Maddie? What if the police just don't know yet?" Wynona's forlorn expression drew sympathy from her friend.

"After school, we'll find out where they took him, and we'll go see him. It was an accident, Wy. You never meant to hit him, did you?"

Wynona shook her head hard and fast. "No! I only wanted to make Jimmy stop hounding me. I would never hurt Mr. Dawson on purpose!"

***

Maddie, Val, and Wynona climbed the steps to St. John's Hospital entrance and headed toward the reception desk. "Can you tell us what room John Dawson is in, please?" Maddie asked.

"John Dawson. Yes, here he is," the receptionist said, tracing her finger down the patient list. "He's in intensive care and not receiving visitors except for immediate family. Do you want me to check his condition?"

"Yes, thanks." Val took charge.

"He's in a coma. There's nothing else noted."

"Thank God," Wynona sighed in relief. Val spun around until she stood face to face with Wynona and grabbed her by the biceps.

"'Thank God?' Do you understand how serious that is?"

Wynona jerked free from Val's grasp. "Well, at least he's not dead!" She stomped off toward the door, but Maddie grabbed her sleeve and pulled her back.

"You need to go tell Mrs. Dawson the whole story of why her husband is here."

In the elevator, Maddie prayed a silent prayer for Mr. Dawson, Mrs. Dawson, and Wynona. When the elevator stopped, Val and Maddie stepped out, but Wynona didn't. "Aren't you coming?" Maddie asked.

"I can't do this," Wynona said, and backed into the corner.

"This is not about you, Wynona," Maddie said. "God says we should love others as much as we love ourselves. So get a grip, and let's go talk to Mrs. Dawson."

Wynona's eyes flared. She sprang into attack mode. "God? You're telling me what God says? Why did God let this happen? Why should I care what He says? He doesn't care about me? You talk as if you and God are on a first name basis. That's insane!"

Maddie didn't flinch. She gazed at Wynona as if seeing her in a new light. "Well, I'm not the one who can't cope, and *we are* on a first name basis. He's the reason the rangers found you so soon. God told me—"

"Sure, He did, Maddie." Her lip curled into a snarl. "You go right ahead and believe that nonsense. I'm not making a fool of myself. You and Val can play Good Samaritan if it makes you feel better. I'll be waiting in the car." Wynona shoved them further away from the elevator and pushed the button to close the door.

"Jeez! What a brat." Val said.

***

"Good afternoon, Mrs. Dawson. I'm Maddie Randall, and this is my friend, Val Michaels. We are in Mr. Dawson's science class."

Mrs. Dawson extended her hand to Maddie, then Val. "You can call me Margaret."

"The receptionist downstairs told us he's in a coma. Has anyone told you how it happened?"

"No. The principal and I spoke in the emergency room, but he didn't give me any details, just that John fell." She tilted her head to the right, raised her eyebrows in question, and waited.

"I was in the lab when it happened," Val said. "He stepped on Wynona Wade's crutch, and it flipped up and hit him in the forehead. He fell backwards into the block wall."

"Oh!" Margaret said, wringing her hands. "John has a head injury from when he was in the army, and he gets dizzy sometimes. I thought that may have been the reason he fell. Thank you for telling me what happened."

"Do you mind if we pray for him?" Maddie asked. "I believe in the power of prayer. Do you?"

She shook her head. "Religion is so illogical. I doubt any of them are worth the trouble."

Maddie intensified her voice. "But Jesus is not a religion. He's God's son."

"I can see your faith is important to you. Thank you for sharing it with me." Margaret gave Maddie a patronizing smile.

"When—if— John wakes up I will tell him you came to see him," she said, then turned to stare out the window.

Val and Maddie left the intensive care unit and headed toward the elevator. "Maddie, do you believe that stuff you told Mrs. Dawson?" Val pushed her hands into her pockets and lifted her shoulders.

"Yes, I believe it, Val. Don't you?"

Val shrugged. "You said He told you where to find Wy. How does He talk to you?"

Maddie hesitated, searching for a word to describe it. "I can't explain it, Val. It's something you have to experience." She pushed the button for ground floor and waited for Val to respond.

"In my family, God has been like a storybook tale. Until you told me about Him talking to you, I never considered that He could be real. That's why I asked your mom to pray."

Maddie nodded. She wondered why she hadn't known that neither Val nor Wynona believed in God. How could she have been so blind?

Wynona was waiting for them in the Carmen Ghia. "You took long enough. Did you talk to Mrs. Dawson?" she asked before they could settle themselves into their seats.

"We did, and we told her how the accident happened. She didn't know about the crutch." Maddie adjusted the rear view mirror before backing out of the parking space.

"So, is she mad?" Wynona's face looked sheepish.

"She is not mad, Wynona. She is grieving and hurting. Mr. Dawson is her husband, and she loves him. You are the last thing on her mind." Val punched the back of the seat with her fist, so close to Wynona's head she flinched and gasped.

"What is wrong with you, Val?"

"Jeez, you really don't have a clue, do you?"

Chapter 6

A receipt for one-hundred forty-three dollars and seventy-nine cents lay on Maddie's pillow, along with a note which read:

This is what it cost me to replace the canvas top on my pontoon boat. I expect to be paid back in thirty days. Leave the keys to your car on the kitchen table. I will hold them as collateral until you pay what you owe.

Maddie crumpled the note, threw it onto the floor and stomped it until it ripped into shreds.

"This is not fair!"

Belva ran into Maddie's room. "Why are you shouting?"

Maddie picked up the bits and pieces of the note, wadded them into a ball and threw them toward the trash can. "Cal replaced that old worn out boat canvas with a brand new one, and it cost over one-hundred and forty-three dollars. I shouldn't have to pay the whole amount. He would have replaced it anyway. I don't have that much money, and he's taking my car keys until I pay him. How can I ever get a job without a car?"

Belva picked up the paper-wad that had bounced off the wall and dropped it into the wastebasket. "I'll talk to him tomorrow about your car, but I can't do anything about the canvas. You disobeyed him when you took the boat without permission."

"I know, but I'll never earn that much money in thirty days. Finding a job could take longer than that." Maddie flopped down on her bed and punched her pillow three times.

"Why don't you sleep on it tonight? We'll pray for an answer. In the morning, things won't be so bleak," Belva said, as she turned back the covers. "Jump into bed. I'll tuck you in."

Maddie crawled into her bed, nested herself into a comfortable position and lay gazing at the ceiling. "Abba, You are asking me to do the impossible. I want to forgive Cal for being mean, but he keeps on poking me, and it makes me angry. Why do I have to be the one to change?" She turned her thoughts back to the note. "Lord, Momma said I should pray about the money I owe him. Will You show me what to do? Please? Amen."

Maddie's eyes popped open before the alarm went off. She had an idea that could solve her problems. After breakfast she tossed her keys onto the kitchen table and ran to catch the school bus. As soon as the bus stopped, she bounded down the steps and dashed to the library to check the job listings on the student information board. Her eyes scanned through several listings before resting on one that interested her. Delighted and excited, she scampered across campus to use the pay phone at the principal's office. The number on the flyer connected her to the personnel supervisor at St. John's Medical Center, who scheduled an appointment with her. Now she needed transportation.

"Val?" Maddie asked in their first period class. "Can you drive me to St. Johns Hospital after school today for a job interview?"

"Why are you looking for a job, Mads? Don't you have enough to do with exams coming up next week?"

"Cal took my car and won't give my keys back until I pay for his new boat canvas. Maybe I can convince him to give back my car so I can drive to work, but first I have to get a job." She looked at Val with anticipation.

"Dad might let me borrow his car to take you over there, but I'd have to ask."

"That's great, Val! Thanks."

After school, Maddie rode the school bus to Val's house.

"We won't be long." Val said. "I will bring the car back as soon as Maddie is finished with her interview." She kissed her dad on the cheek and he kissed her back. Maddie envied her.

"Thanks, Mr. Michaels."

"Wish me well," Maddie said as she headed toward the hospital entrance. Her hands trembled from excitement and anticipation.

"Please let this work out, Abba," she prayed as she walked.

"Good afternoon, Miss Randall. I'm Sarah with hospital personnel. Thank you for applying with us. Let me look over your application and then we can talk job details and qualifications. Please have a seat."

Maddie smiled and sat in the chair in front of the desk. She surveyed the walls while she waited for Sarah's cue. Photos of stiff-necked hospital administrators and somber-faced doctors lined the gray walls. She wondered if working in the medical field caused people to be unhappy, or was that look supposed to be professional?

"I see you've had experience as a waitress, so you've worked with the public. That's good. This job is to assist nurses, and requires interaction with patients and hospital staff. Our goal is to hire students interested in healthcare professions, so the hours are flexible to accommodate your school schedule."

"I haven't decided what I'll do after graduation, but working in health care is a good choice. This job will help me make that decision."

Sarah smiled and nodded. "I like your attitude, Maddie, but I have three other applicants to interview before I decide. If hired, you will work from four-thirty until eight-thirty p.m. on Mondays, Tuesdays, and Thursdays, and Saturdays from eight a.m. until noon. The pay is minimum wage."

Maddie did a mental calculation. *Sixteen hours at $1.60 per hour---that's twenty-five dollars and sixty cents a week. After taxes, that's twenty-three dollars, times four weeks. I could earn ninety-two dollars, and there's forty dollars in my savings account, but I'll need gasoline. If Mrs. Cooper will let me babysit, that might make up the difference.*

"Thank you, Sarah. I'd love to take the position."

Sarah gave her a professional smile, a handshake and a pleasant nod toward the door. "I will let you know by Friday afternoon."

It seemed to Maddie that she had packed a year's worth of waiting into the space of one week. When it arrived, she could hardly wait to get home to find out if Sarah had called.

She ran home from the bus stop without stopping to chat with Uncle Josh, who waved to her from his front porch. His stories and jokes made her laugh, even when he told the same ones over and over. But today she didn't take time to visit because she hoped she had good news waiting for her at home.

"Did Sarah call from the hospital?" She bopped through the backdoor, knocking Belva backwards.

"Slow down, Maddie," Belva said, grabbing at the counter to keep from falling.

"I'm sorry, Momma. This week has lasted an eternity."

Belva motioned for Maddie to sit. She placed a plate of crackers and peanut butter and a glass of milk on the table and sat in the chair next to her. "Sarah called at two-thirty this afternoon. Do you want to know what she said?"

"Don't torture me, Momma. Please, please, please, tell me."

Belva tapped her fingers against her chin. "I should wait until you finish your crackers. I don't want you to get choked."

Maddie laid the cracker on the plate and brushed the crumbs off her fingers. "I won't take another bite until you tell me. Is it good news or bad?"

"Both. Which do you want first?"

"Bad news first, then the good, I guess."

Belva frowned and said, "The bad news is, you didn't get the job you wanted."

Maddie felt her smile turn upside down. She couldn't believe she had waited all week for bad news.

"What is the good news?" she asked, not caring now.

A wide grin on Belva's face encouraged Maddie. "The good news is, they want you to take another position with higher pay and a few extra hours each week!" She clapped her hands and giggled at the prank she had just played on Maddie. "I'm sorry, but I had to tease you."

Maddie's face beamed. "Are you serious? They want me? Thank you, God!" She popped out of her chair and jumped up and down, clapping her hands with excitement. "That's so wonderful! What is the job? How much more does it pay?"

"She said two dollars an hour and twenty hours a week. You'll be a patient aide."

Maddie felt the love when a heightened look of pride spread across Belva's face.

"That means I can get Cal paid back in thirty days and have money left over. Yes! Yes! Yes!" Maddie danced around the room in delight. "Now, if I can convince Cal to give back my keys, my problem is solved."

Maddie awoke on Saturday morning, eager for Cal to get out of bed. Most weekends she hoped he slept the entire day, but today she needed to talk to him. She went outside to the front porch after breakfast and waited, hoping he didn't wake up grumpy.

"Maddie," the soft voice whispered.

"Yes, Abba."

"I gave you the job at the hospital because I have a special favor to ask. Will you do it?"

"I'll try, Abba. What do you want me to do?"

"Go to John Dawson and pray for his healing while you are visiting him."

"Okay, Abba, if I can. Mrs. Dawson won't like it."

The voice faded when Belva came to the door and motioned her to come in. "Cal is up and ready for breakfast if you want to talk to him."

"Okay, Momma. I'm coming. Is he in a good mood today?"

"It will be fine, Maddie. Come on inside." She followed Belva to the kitchen where Cal sat flipping through the morning newspaper.

"Good morning, Daddy. May I get you more coffee?"

"Are you trying to get out of paying for the canvas? Because if you are, it won't work," Cal folded the paper and laid it aside. "But I will take another half-cup."

"I'm not trying to get out of it. I got a job working at the hospital after school and on Saturdays, so I can pay. At least, I can if you let me drive over there. Without my car, I can't take the job. Could I give you something else for collateral, or make it up to you another way?" She set his cup on the table in front of him and held her breath, waiting for his answer.

Cal reared back in his chair and gave her a surprised look. "So, you got a job. I will make a deal with you, Maddie. You can drive your car to work and back, but no further until your debt is paid. In exchange for the privilege, you clean my car inside and out and put a coat of wax on it. Will you agree to that?"

"I can do that," she said, but she dreaded the task. Cal never cleaned his car. The floor mats had soil embedded in the fibers from his work boots. The exterior was so deep with mud and grime she would have to spend the entire afternoon getting it clean. But it was the price she would pay to get her keys back.

Monday afternoon at 4:30 on the dot, Maddie punched the clock in the employee lounge at St. John's Hospital. Her first assignment was to take a discharged patient to the front entrance. "This should be easy," she thought.

She grabbed a wheelchair from the equipment supply room and pushed it down the hall to Room 423. The discharge order read James Smith, bed two. "Good afternoon, Mr. Smith," Maddie said in her most cheerful voice while backing the wheelchair into the room and parking it at the foot of bed two.

"Good afternoon to you, young lady." A deep masculine voice resounded from the chair in the corner. Maddie spun around startled. She had expected Mr. Smith to be in bed. And she never imagined him to be so—big.

"I'm Maddie. I'm here to take you to your car. Are you ready?" That's what she said, but what she thought was, *"Oh, my Lord, have mercy, this man must weigh four-hundred pounds. I hope I can do this!"*

Mr. Smith leaned his weight against her and struggled to get to his feet. "Whoa, Mr. Smith. I need help to get you into that chair. I'll be right back."

Maddie went to the nurses' station to ask for help. "He's heavier than I can manage by myself," she said to the floor nurse on duty.

"Sweetie, I can't help you. I have an emergency in room 407. Pick up the phone and dial three-zero. Ask for Frankie. He's the orderly on duty tonight."

"Sure, okay. Thanks," Maddie said as the nurse ran toward the room with the red light flashing above the door.

She picked up the receiver and dialed. A kind, upbeat voice answered on the other end. "You have reached Frankie Mason. Please key in your number."

"Number? What number?" Maddie scanned the nurse's desk for answers. It could be the room number, or the station number. "Oh, pooh, what do I do now?" She was still murmuring when someone tapped her on the shoulder from behind.

"Are you the damsel in distress?"

Maddie turned around, startled. "I suppose so. Who are you?"

"I'm Frankie. I believe you paged me."

"Uh, hi, Frankie, my name is Maddie. I'm the new aide. Are you the person to call for help with loading a patient? Mr. Smith in room 423 is going home today. I need help to get him into the wheelchair." she said to the muscular, black-haired, blue-eyed hunk standing beside her. "How did you get here so fast? I didn't even enter the number."

"A pleasure to meet you, Maddie," Frankie said, flashing a delightful smile. "I was in the lounge next door when I heard you mumbling. I figured I should just come on over and help you out."

"Thank you, Frankie. It's a pleasure to meet you too."

He pretended to tip an imaginary hat with his right hand and motioned towards Mr. Smith's room with the left. "Shall we go move a patient, Maddie?"

Mr. Smith had grown weary of waiting and attempted to put himself into the wheelchair, but instead, had ended up on the floor.

"I guess I missed the mark," he said when Frankie and Maddie walked into the room.

"Oh! My! Mr. Smith, are you okay?"

"I will be as soon as I get my blubber bottom off the floor and into that chair," he laughed. "I still haven't learned the virtue of patience. Do you suppose you two could help me in recovering from this most embarrassing predicament?" He extended both hands for them to pull him off the floor.

"I'll go for a patient lift, Mr. Smith. Just stay put and I'll be right back," Frankie said.

"'Stay put,' he says." Mr. Smith laughed harder. "As if I had a choice. ,"

Frankie came back with the lift and positioned it between the bed and the wall behind Mr. Smith. "Okay, sir. If you're ready, Miss Maddie and I will work this lift beneath you, but we need you to help us. Can you rock yourself from side to side when I ask you to?"

"I will give it my best effort, young man. Say when."

On Frankie's command, Mr. Smith leaned to the right, raising his left side off the floor enough for Frankie to slide the lift seat beneath him. "Now lean to the left, sir." Mr. Smith obliged by leaning his head into Maddie's legs for support. Unprepared for the weight, she leaned forward for balance. His head came to rest on her bosom and he sighed a pleasurable, "Aaah!"

"I'm so sorry, sir." Maddie apologized, trying to hide her embarrassment.

"No need to apologize, Miss Maddie. It has been a long time since anyone held me so close." He grinned and chuckled. "May we try that again?"

Frankie's face looked contorted, and he wiped it with his sleeve, trying to hide the grin so Maddie wouldn't see him laughing. "Let's get you off the floor," he said, struggling to sober his voice.

"Okay, on the count of three, I'll start the lift and Maddie will steady the seat. Place your hands on the support bars and try to keep yourself as steady as you can. Is everybody ready?"

"Ready," Maddie and Mr. Smith chimed together.

"One, two, three!" Frankie started the hydraulics. Inch by inch, four-hundred pounds of patient rose into the air and swayed from side to side like a car headed for the crusher. Maddie guided the lift toward the wheelchair and centered Mr. Smith above the seat. The lift whirred when Frankie reversed directions and lowered him onto the chair.

"That's the most fun I've had in decades." Mr. Smith laughed out loud.

While Frankie returned the lift to the supply room, Maddie loaded Mr. Smith's belongings onto the wheelchair. She grabbed the hand grips and pushed with all her might, but the chair didn't budge. Mr. Smith gave the wheels a forward push and got it moving. They made it to the elevator before Frankie showed up again to help.

He stood behind Maddie and placed his hands over hers to take the chair. Maddie squirmed and felt the warmth in her cheeks from the blush she knew was there. She lingered a second to savor the warmth of his body against her back and the essence of his pheromones mingled with expensive cologne.

He kept his hands in place over hers and waited for her to turn loose of the chair, but she held tight. "No, I've got this," she said. "Thank you for helping me put Mr. Smith in the chair, but it's my job."

"Are you sure? I'm here to help." He backed away and searched her eyes.

"I'm positive," Maddie said, even though she wasn't. "But thank you for asking."

She wheeled the chair into the elevator and pushed the button for the ground floor. Mr. Smith's face, reflected in the shiny metal door, showed a twinkle in his eye and a mischievous smile. He uttered a sensual *mmmm* and licked his upper lip.

"He's remembering sticking his face into my chest," Maddie thought, and shuddered at what he might be imagining.

When they arrived at Patient Loading, she pushed the chair through the automatic doors onto the walkway. She unloaded his belongings, but forgot to set the handbrake. The chair began to roll.

"No! Wait!" Maddie squealed and flung his duffle bag onto the sidewalk. She ran toward the chair, tripped over the bag, and fell into Mr. Smith's lap. The chair rolled faster down the ramp. "Help! Somebody help!" The chair picked up speed until the front wheels spun around and banged against the curb on the opposite side of the driveway. The sudden stop threw Maddie off his lap. She landed bottom first in the fountain, arms and legs splayed in four directions with the fountain spray bouncing off her head like rain splatting on concrete.

"Are you all right, honey?" Mr. Smith called from his ringside seat, slapping his hands against his thighs, and laughing so hard his chubby cheeks jiggled. "Oh!" he shouted. "I've just had a tonsillectomy! It hurts." But he kept on laughing.

Maddie stood and rubbed her bottom then squeezed the water from her soggy ponytail. Her shoes squeaked when she padded over to Mr. Smith, blubbering, and said, "Are you okay sir? I'm so sorry."

"I'm just dandy," he said, still struggling to control his laughter. "You're the most excitement I've had in forty years."

When Maddie was sure she couldn't be any more embarrassed, Frankie walked up behind Mr. Smith's chair and wheeled him back up the ramp. He gave her a wide grin, shook his head, and said, "You sure are pretty, Miss Maddie."

Chapter 7

The next morning, Maddie joined Wynona and Val on the back seat of the school bus. "Did you see Mr. Dawson yesterday, Mads?" Val asked.

"No, but I plan to this afternoon. I'm scheduled to work the third floor today. That's where they took him after releasing him from intensive care."

"Is he still comatose?" Wynona applied lipstick to her bottom lip and rubbed her lips together. "He's such a science nerd. That bump on the head may have improved his personality." She snickered as if the whole incident were a joke.

"There's nothing funny about Mr. Dawson being in a coma," Maddie said.

"Yeah," Val said, "If he dies, you could go to prison for manslaughter. I doubt you would laugh then. You're such a goat."

"Listen to the little Miss Goody Two-Shoes twins. You're not so perfect yourselves."

When the bus rolled into the school parking lot, Maddie rose from her seat and strode toward the open door. *I can live without all the drama,* she thought.

At the hospital that afternoon, Maddie went to visit the Dawsons. She popped her head into the room and said, "Hello, Margaret. Do you remember me---Maddie Randall? Val and I came by to visit last week."

Margaret frowned. "Yes, I remember you. You're the girl who believes prayer makes a difference." Her eyes had dark circles beneath them, and she looked like she hadn't slept in days.

"That's the reason I came by today. I want to stand by Mr. Dawson's bed and pray for him if you don't mind."

Margaret frowned and shook her head. "Well, I mind. My husband is in a coma. Don't you get it? He can't hear, he can't speak, he can't respond and he's not aware he exists. Mumbling over John won't change that. Go away!" She led Maddie to the door and slammed it behind her.

Maddie leapt forward when the door banged into her backside.

***

"The patient in room 312 needs help to get to the bathroom, Maddie," the supervising nurse said, and pointed to the flashing light over the door.

"Yes, ma'am." Maddie hurried off down the hall wondering how she could do what Abba asked when Margaret wouldn't let her.

Two hours later, she passed by his door and noticed Margaret was not with her husband. She looked both ways down the hallway, then slipped inside and shut the door. With her left hand around John Dawson's forearm and her right hand over his heart, she prayed.

"Dear Abba,
You asked me to pray for Mr. Dawson, and I believe You hear me. Please touch him and heal him. If it's Your will, please wake him up and make him well again. Mrs. Dawson doesn't believe in You, Abba, but I hope she will. Will You please put a longing in her heart to seek for You, and help her believe? And, Abba, please help Wynona and Val too.
Amen"

Margaret opened the door. "I thought I told you to leave!" She shouted at Maddie, waving her hands in the air and shooing her away from the bedside. Then she collapsed on her husband's bed, laid her head on his legs, and sobbed. Maddie waited in silence until she lifted her head. The heaviness in her face reflected the painful emptiness in her soul. "Go home, Miss Randall."
When her shift ended, Maddie pushed her luck and stopped by to check on Margaret. The door stood ajar. Maddie knocked twice and opened it wider.

"May I come in, Margaret?" she asked, keeping her voice low.

"Come in, come in!" she said, sounding so light-hearted and pleasant that Maddie wondered if she had taken stimulants. "There's good news! John's awake."

"Praise the Lord!" Maddie forgot she was in the hospital and let out a loud whoop. "Thank you, Abba!"

Margaret gave her a quizzical look. "Who is Abba?"

"Oh! Margaret! He is the Father, the Son, and the Holy Spirit. I call him Abba."

"You speak about God in such a personal way."

"Jesus wants us to be close to Him, and He told me to come in here and stand by Mr. Dawson's bed and pray for him. When you ran me out earlier I didn't know how I could, but when I came back later and you weren't here, I figured it was my chance. I'm sorry I offended you, but I had to do what He asked me to do so Mr. Dawson can get well."

Margaret shook her head, grinning. "I thought you'd never come up for air, Maddie. I don't know how you have so much faith in something you can't see. I don't know if that's what made John wake up, but if it did, then I'm so happy you do. You've been nothing but kind and supportive, and I don't deserve your forgiveness, but will you forgive me for being rude to you earlier?" Her eyes gleamed with sincerity and hope.

Maddie shrugged her shoulders. "It's okay. I never got mad at you. I'm glad he's getting better."

"Thank you, Maddie."

"Thank you, Abba, for answering my prayer for Mr. Dawson."

Chapter 8

Thirty-two dollars and twenty-nine cents. Maddie counted the money from her secret envelope hidden in her winter coat pocket in the back of the closet. Twenty-four days left before she had to pay Cal in full. She needed thirty-seven dollars and seventeen-cents each week for the next three weeks. "I should put some of this in the collection plate on Sunday. But if I do, I won't have enough." She put the money back into her coat pocket.

"Give from your heart, Maddie," Abba spoke.

***

Her second week at St. John's started out easy. No one seemed to know about the mishap with Mr. Smith. For sure, she would never forget to set the handbrake on a wheelchair again.

Frankie walked up behind her at the nurse's station. "I have Friday evening off, Maddie. May I take you out for a soda after you finish your shift?"

"I—I don't know. Exams are next week and I need to study."

"We won't stay out late, I promise. Just a soda. You are the most fascinating person I've met in a long time. I'd love to get to know you better."

He brushed her hair off her shoulder with his hand and let it linger a second against her neck.

"You must meet plenty of older girls who are much more interesting than I am. I'm still in high school and you're in pre-med. I can't imagine we have much in common." She pulled her hair back over her shoulder.

"Ah yes, older perhaps, but not as captivating. Allow me until Friday before you say no. I won't give up until you give me a fair chance. If we don't find something in common by then, I won't ask again. What do you say?"

"I doubt if I can stop you from trying, but you're wasting your time." She picked up her work schedule from the desk. "My dad is strict, and I'm semi-grounded for destroying his boat canvas."

He tucked his hands into his lab coat pockets and raised his eyebrows with two quick ticks. "So, you're saying you want to—but your Dad won't let you?"

"That is not what I said." A smile crept across her lips. She couldn't ignore the cute dimple in his left cheek and the five o'clock shadow forming around his chin.

Frankie looked hopeful. "So you're grounded for destroying a boat canvas? Does that mean you like boats? Looks like we've already found a common interest. Maybe you will tell me the rest of the story on Friday?" Frankie swayed as he walked away whistling the theme song from the movie *Midnight Cowboy*.

***

Maddie grabbed the phone off the end table as soon as she got home and carried it into her bedroom, dragging the twenty-five-foot long connection cord behind her. She kicked off her shoes, flung herself across her bed and called Val. "I have something exciting to tell you. Can you come over here?"

"Not tonight, Mads. I need to study."

"I met this guy at the hospital. He is handsome, and he's in pre-med. He asked me to go out with him." Her heart beat a little faster.

"Mads! An older man! What are you thinking? You're not going out with him are you? Your daddy will string you up like a sausage and have you for breakfast."

"I know, but Frankie is nice. I can't believe he's interested in me." She wound and unwound the phone cord around her finger until it curled into a tangled knot.

"I know what you're thinking, Mads. If you sneak around Cal and do this behind his back, you're stirring in the outhouse hole. I hope you grow some sense in your head tonight while you're sleeping. I have to go now," Val said, "but I'll see you at lunch tomorrow."

"Bye, Val." Maddie flipped through her record collection and found the soundtrack from *Midnight Cowboy*. She set the turntable arm to replay and played it over and over until she fell asleep dreaming of Frankie's blue eyes and dimpled smile.

***

"Are you still thinking of going out with that older fellow you met at the hospital, Maddie?" Val asked while they waited in the cafeteria line.

"What did you say? Maddie is dating an older man? Tell me more!" Wynona huddled closer, itching to hear.

"No." Maddie whispered. "I haven't been out with him, but he asked me out for a soda after work next Friday."

"How old is he? Is he handsome? He's not married, is he? Oh, shame on you." Wynona crooked her right index finger and wiggled it at Maddie.

"His name is Frankie Mason. He's an orderly at St. John's hospital. He is not married, and yes, he is dreamy handsome with raven hair, blue eyes, and the cutest dimple in his left cheek when he smiles. I'm afraid if I go out with him, I might lose control, attack and devour him---he looks so delicious." Maddie licked her lips and fanned her face, teasing Wynona's over-eager appetite.

"You should go, Maddie. He can get you into clubs and parties, and you could sample those exotic drinks with the little umbrellas. I wish an older man would ask me out. I'd love to experiment a little with adulthood, if you know what I mean." She winked and purred like a kitten getting a belly rub.

"He might be a rapist, or an ax murderer who preys on the innocent and leaves them chopped into bits in the wood shed. He *is* studying the human body. What better way to learn the inner workings of humankind than by taking it apart piece by piece?" Val stood toe-to-toe and head-to-head with Wynona, looking cross-eyed at her nose. "But I can see you are not innocent, so too bad he won't be looking for you."

"Stop it," Maddie pretended to swat them with her tray. "He's not an ax murderer, and I'm not interested in experimenting with anything *adult*. Besides, Cal would never allow me to date a twenty-four-year-old. I'll never get my car back if I get into more trouble."

Wynona shrugged. "You're such a do-gooder, Maddie. You stay in trouble with Cal anyway, so you might as well have fun."

Val rolled her eyes, and Wynona picked up an apple from the bar, held it between her teeth, and hobbled away on her crutches. "If you're sitting with her, Maddie, I'm sitting somewhere else. Call me when you get home tonight."

CHAPTER 9

On Friday evening, Maddie smiled when she read her paycheck. Pay to the order of Maddie Randall the sum of forty dollars and fifty-nine cents. The two additional hours she had worked last Saturday paid off well. She should put the extra in the collection plate on Sunday, but if she saved it, she could get her car back sooner.

"What are you contemplating, Maddie Randall? You can't stare at your paycheck and will it to grow."

"Hi, Frankie. I wish you were a master money wizard. I'd ask you to grant me enough cash to pay back the one-hundred and forty-three dollars I still owe Cal." She folded her check and shoved it into her pocket. "Then I could get my car back."

"Didn't you drive a brown Carmen Ghia onto the parking lot this afternoon? Isn't that your car?" Frankie followed her to the time clock and punched her time card into the slot.

"It is, but I can only drive it to work and back. To make it the story short, three weeks ago I took Cal's boat out without his permission and got caught out on the lake in a storm. The old worn-out tarp he used as a cover got ripped. The only reason he lets me drive the car to work is so I can earn enough to pay for a new one."

He tapped her on the elbow. "You could tell me the long version of that story over that soda I promised you."

"I need to go home, Frankie. If I'm late, Cal will swear I've been driving to places other than work. Thank you though. I love talking to you." She turned and hurried toward the elevator.

He skipped to catch up with her. "Okay then. What if I buy you a soda and walk you to your car?"

"You are mighty persistent, Frankie Mason. How can I resist such charm? I am a little thirsty."

Frankie sprinted to the lounge and back again. He popped the top on her soda and slid the back of his hand across her arm before placing the can in her palm. She shuddered when chills trickled down her neck.

"I didn't mean to offend you, Maddie. You're hard to resist."

"No. The soda is cold. It gave me a chill." She lied and looked away.

At the car, Frankie took her keys, unlocked her door, and helped her into the driver's seat. They lingered, talking and flirting, until the shadows crept over the parking lot and the street light on the corner flickered on. She was late.

***

Maddie drove home faster than usual and ran from her car to the house. "I'm sorry I'm late, Momma. I was talking to a friend, and time got away from me. It won't happen again, I promise."

Belva wrinkled her forehead and sighed. "Cal called at nine o'clock and asked for you. I couldn't lie to him, Maddie. You should have let me know where you were."

"Oh, no." Maddie flopped herself onto the sofa and whined. "I'm always home on time. Why did he choose tonight to check up on me?" Her heart fluttered and her hands shook when she remembered---tomorrow is Saturday and Cal will be home. "He won't believe me!"

Saturday morning, Maddie left home earlier than usual. She couldn't clock in before her scheduled work time, but at least she wouldn't have to face Cal before he had his morning coffee.

Margaret Dawson was in the doorway of her husband's hospital room when Maddie came down the hallway. "Good morning, Maddie," she beamed and waved Maddie closer. "I haven't seen you in a few days. I thought you had forgotten us."

"No, Margaret. I didn't forget, just been busy. I got here before my shift starts, so I thought I'd drop by. How is he doing?"

"Maddie, he is great. The doctor says he can go home today. Thank you again for what you've done. I know I told you I didn't believe in prayer, but after seeing how much better John is since you prayed for him, I'm almost convinced you're right."

Maddie looked upward and mouthed a silent thank you. "That's wonderful, Margaret. I hope you will ask Jesus to help you believe, then you can help someone else. May I see Mr. Dawson?"

"You may. Please come in."

John grinned and held out his arms for Maddie to give him a hug. She hesitated a moment, not sure if she should hug a teacher, until Margaret patted her on the shoulder and urged her forward.

"Come here, young lady, and let me thank you." He laughed and cried when he pulled Maddie into a massive hug. "Margaret told me how you've prayed for me and encouraged her. She has struggled with doubt since we lost our son in Vietnam. Before, she went to church every Sunday and prayed every day for Johnny to make it home, but when that didn't happen she became angry with God. I think she just stopped believing at all when it looked like she was losing me too. She's finding her faith again because of you. Thank you, Maddie Randall." John grabbed her hand and patted it.

"Will you be back at school soon?"

"I'm taking a leave of absence for the rest of this term, but I plan to be there for the next one. I hope you'll drop by the lab, and please tell your friend Wynona she's not to blame. The fall didn't cause the coma. In fact, it probably saved my life. The doctors said if I hadn't fallen, they wouldn't have found the clot in time. I might have died."

Maddie looked at her wrist watch. "I'll make sure she knows, but now I have to go clock in."

Margaret walked her to the door. "We'll never forget you, Maddie," she said.

She skipped away humming. "Thank you, Abba."

***

Cal met Maddie in the driveway, stuck out his hand and said "I'll take those keys now, young lady."

"What? Why? I haven't driven the car anywhere except to work and—"

"So you say." His gray-blue eyes burned into her. "Don't even bother telling me where you were yesterday evening at nine o'clock. I don't want to hear any more of your lies. Give me the keys now!"

"Give me a chance to explain! I can't pay for the tarp if I don't work, and I can't just quit my job without giving notice. Please, Cal." Her voice trembled and her eyes flooded, spilling tears onto the steering wheel.

Cal jerked open the door and pulled her out of the car. "Shut up and go in the house. You won't be driving for a long time."

Anger raged inside Maddie. *I hate you, Cal Randall*, she said in her heart again.

***

"I need a favor," Maddie said at lunch the next day.

"What do you need?" Wynona and Val both volunteered.

"I need you to go over to St. John's and take this letter to my supervisor. Cal took my keys again because he thought I drove somewhere after work. I didn't, but he never gave me a chance to explain. I don't want to quit my job without an explanation. Will you give it to the evening supervisor who's on staff tonight?"

"Of course we will, Maddie. Does this mean you won't be talking to Frankie anymore?" Wynona asked. "Because if you're not, I could look him up and tell him why you're not coming back to work." She winked at Val.

"Thanks, but no thanks," Maddie said. "But if you should run into him while you're there, will you give him this note for me?" She held in her hand a folded sheet of pink stationary. Val stepped between Wynona and Maddie and took the note. "That will be my pleasure," she said, and jabbed her elbow into Wynona's rib.

Chapter 10

"Abba, are you listening? I don't understand. When I've done my best, I still get in trouble with Cal. Why won't he be reasonable?" Her thoughts turned from prayer to anger. "I thought You said You loved me and would never leave me! Why didn't You stop him from taking my car? I am not giving him my money! Wynona is right! Cal blames me for things I haven't done, so I might as well do them!" She never waited for His response. Instead she picked up the phone and dialed.

"Hi, Wynona, did you and Val meet Frankie?"

"Yes, we did, you lucky woman. We met him in the elevator on the way up to the fourth floor. Those blue eyes are intoxicating." She topped off her enthusiasm with a gleeful, "Yummy!"

Maddie ignored Wynona's overtones. "Did you give him my note?"

"Yeah. He looked disappointed when we told him you weren't coming back to work." Wynona said. "He folded the note and put it in his pocket, so he'll probably," her voice lilted in soprano, "call you."

"I sure hope Cal isn't here when he calls." Maddie said. "I don't want him to know about Frankie."

"If he asks you out, how are you going to go out with him and still keep him secret?" Wynona asked, her wiles undisguised.

"You and Val are my friends. Can't I trust you to help us hook up?" Maddie's disclosure of her plans to defy Cal boosted Wynona's sassiness.

"I don't know about Val, but you can count on me, girl!" Wynona hooted.

Maddie chuckled. "He thinks he can control me, but he is oh so wrong!"

***

Three days had gone by and Frankie hadn't called. She blamed Cal. If he hadn't demanded she give up her job, Frankie might have asked her out again. Now she would always wonder.

After exams on Friday, she set off for the library. Her mind wandered into *what if* land where Cal became a loving and supportive dad and … A toot-toot startled her when she stepped off the curb into oncoming traffic.

"Watch where you're going!" She yelled at the driver, knowing he wasn't at fault.

"Someone should," a recognizable voice yelled back. "Where were you going with your head in the clouds, Miss Randall?"

Maddie shaded her eyes from the glare and peered through the front window of a red convertible sports car. Behind the wheel sat Frankie, wearing a grin as wide as the windshield of his tiny car. "What are you—? I'm so sor— I wasn't paying atten—." Horns blared and drivers stuck their heads out of windows screaming, "Get out of the road, idiot!"

Frankie leaned over and opened the passenger side door. "What were you thinking, wandering out into traffic that way, Maddie? I could have run over you."

She jumped backward out of the street and climbed in. "A better question might be, what are you doing over on the east side of town? I thought you lived on the west side."

"You should be glad I'm on the east side, otherwise you would be road kill smeared all over the bumper of that pickup truck behind me." Frankie reached across the console and slipped his hand into hers and squeezed.

"It's good to see you, Maddie. Your friends told me you weren't coming back to work because your Dad took your car. I'm sorry I kept you too long, talking."

"It's not your fault, Frankie. Cal looks for ways to torment me." She looked at him and rolled her eyes.

"He must be crazy to be mean to a sweetheart like you." Frankie took his eyes off the road to look at her and ran his tire into the ditch.

"Look out! There's a telephone pole!" Maddie screamed the instant he swerved the car back onto the road.

He leaned his head back and yelled "Yeeow!" then pushed the accelerator to the floor and held it there, not letting off until the road curved ahead of them. After the curve, he pulled over onto the shoulder and leaned across the console. He ran his fingers underneath Maddie's hair at the back of her neck and pulled her into his kiss.

Maddie leaned into him then pulled back when she realized she liked it way too much. "What are you doing, Frankie? Are you always so impulsive?"

"No, not always. You make me crazy, Maddie. I apologize. I shouldn't have kissed you without asking first." His face lingered above hers. She felt the warmth of his breath on her cheek.

She squirmed and pushed her head against the headrest, widening the space between them. "I've never had so much excitement in a single afternoon. I need to catch my breath."

He moved away and settled himself in the driver's seat. "Can we start over with a slower beat?"

"No," she said shaking her head. "Let's just slow the beat and move forward."

"I like you, Maddie." Frankie started the engine. "May I drive you home?"

"Not today, Frankie. But, call me later?"

He let her out at the front of the school library and cruised away, whistling.

Wynona came out of the library just in time to see his car pulling away. "Did I see what I thought I saw?" She furrowed her brow and tucked her chin.

"If you saw Frankie driving away, then I guess you did. He came by to apologize," Maddie was still watching his brake lights as he turned the corner at the end of the block.

"Apologize? For what?"

"We were talking in the parking lot after work Friday, and I got home late. That's the reason Cal took my keys again."

"Uh-huh. So he drove over here to apologize when he could have called?"

Maddie couldn't hold back her smile. "Maybe," she sighed. "May-be."

Chapter 11

The phone rang and Maddie jumped off the sofa to grab it. "I'll get it!"

"Hello?"

"Hello, Maddie. This is Frankie. May I come over?"

"Um– that's not a good idea. I haven't told Momma or Cal about you yet. Can you meet me at Burke Elementary School just below our house?"

"I can be there in fifteen minutes."

"I'll meet you there," she whispered into the phone.

On the back porch, Belva was peeling potatoes for dinner. Maddie came outside and grabbed her basketball from the wooden crate beneath the window where she'd left it last. "I'm meeting Wynona and Val at the elementary school to shoot hoops, Momma."

"Okay, Maddie, but be back before dark." She hummed snippets of hymns as she worked. Each note ignited a spark of guilt in Maddie's conscience.

Maddie kissed Belva on the cheek and remembered Judas, the disciple who betrayed Jesus. But that didn't stop her.

When Frankie pulled into the parking lot, she motioned him to drive around to the back of the building.

"Why so clandestine?" he asked. "Your mom can't see the school from your house."

"No, but Aunt Ruby can. She lives right across the road and she has a curiosity problem."

He parked the car out of sight and met Maddie on the basketball court.

"How about a game of horse?" Maddie bounced the ball and bobbed back and forth to keep it under control.

"Okay, but I warn you, I hold the title for stomping the most toes in the history of West High."

Maddie giggled and tossed the basketball to him. "Show me your stuff, mister."

He bounced the ball three times and waltzed it toward her, stopping in front of her with his arms raised high. He tossed the ball toward the goal then let his arms fall around her as it passed through the hoop. "May I please kiss you, Maddie?"

Maddie leaned in and lifted her face. His muscles flexed when he tightened his arms and pulled her closer. Minty breath and scented aftershave stirred a brief memory of Granny Nettie's aromatic herb garden that morphed into a warm, seductive fog when he lowered his lips to hers. She lingered a moment, enveloped in his passion, then broke the kiss, but didn't move away. Her body trembled. He balanced his chin against the top of her head, and they embraced in silence until she stopped trembling and pushed him away.

She moved to the sideline, picked up the basketball and tossed it through the hoop. Frankie caught it and passed it back to her.

"I've never had such intense feelings before, Frankie. I'm so–confused." She traced the imprinted lettering with her thumb, then placed the ball on the ground when he reached for her hands.

"You don't have to do anything you don't want to do," he said. The sensuous warmth in her fingertips inched its way throughout her body, and she pulled herself free from his grasp. She pressed the heels of her hands to her forehead. "I don't know what I want. God is on my right shoulder and the devil is on my left, and they are battling it out between my ears." She shook her head to clear her mind.

"Do you believe in that spiritual stuff?" Frankie slinked away from her and shook his head.

"I do." She questioned him with her eyes. "Don't you, Frankie?"

He shrugged and looked away. "I don't know. That part about a virgin having a baby—I have a hard time with that."

"Why?" She gestured her wonderment with upturned palms. "If God made the first man from scratch, then He could make another one without the help of a man."

"You are too much, Maddie Randall." Frankie laughed. "I guess you made a good point."

"I have to go now," she said. "The sun is going down, and I promised Momma I'd be back before dark." Frankie moved back into her personal space and bent to kiss her again, but she backed away and picked up her basketball. "Good night, Frankie," she said and ran toward Burke Road without looking back.

***

"Did Frankie call you?" Wynona asked first thing when Maddie boarded the school bus the next morning. Maddie picked up the pencil that had fallen from her math book onto the floor.

"Mr. Dawson wanted me to tell you you're not responsible for his coma. The bump from the fall didn't even make a pump knot. The doctors found a blood clot from an old head injury that might have killed him if they hadn't examined him when they did. So I guess you're cleared," Maddie said.

"Wow! First I thought I'd killed him, and now I'm a hero. I'm glad I didn't listen to you two and make a fool of myself in front of Mrs. Dawson. I did nothing wrong."

Val put her hands on her hips in a defiant posture. "Yes, you did something wrong! Just because you got lucky, and it turned out good for you doesn't make it right for you to pretend it didn't happen. You still need to apologize to him."

"I am not apologizing to Mr. Dawson. Jimmy Jones is the one who needs to apologize to him, and to me. This was his fault."

"Jeez, I can't believe you, Wynona," Val said.

"Who asked for your opinion, Val?" Wynona turned to Maddie. "You still haven't answered my question, did Frankie call you?"

"Are you jealous, Wynona? I'm wondering if you want him to call you instead."

"Well, I wouldn't hang up on him if he did. I hope you are woman enough to appreciate what you have."

"What's wrong with you?" Val moved in front of Wynona. "Since you broke your ankle, you've been impossible."

"Hey, *no need for good stuff to go to waste* is my motto." Wynona turned her back to Val and said to Maddie, "If you don't want him, I'll take him off your hands. After the storm, I decided to go after whatever I want. I could have died out there, and I want to have fun while I still can."

"Shut up, Wy," Val snapped. "You're circling like a vulture waiting for a tiger to ditch its prey."

Maddie tossed her books on the seat in front of them and listened to them bicker all the way to school. She was glad Wynona hadn't pushed harder for details about last night.

***

All day long, Maddie struggled. The memory of Frankie, the smell of his skin, his dimpled smile, and the way he had kissed her with such gentle passion distracted her. She wanted to ask Abba for help, but He would send her to the Bible again. She hadn't forgotten what He had told her about love. Frankie didn't love her, and she didn't love him, but the lure of possibility drew her. She didn't want to let go of this feeling. Not yet.

"Come to me, Maddie." Abba's gentle voice beckoned her to safety, but she didn't go.

CHAPTER 12

Val's face beamed when she told Maddie the news. "The swim team took first place in the regionals, and we will go to the state competition in the fall! Woohoo! I can't believe we beat Asner County! They've taken the state championship three years in a row." She pounded both fists against her locker door then pranced around in a victory dance. "You'll be at the celebration party Friday evening at Mountainside Park, won't you, Mads? I mean—I know you're grounded from driving, but will Cal let you come if I pick you up?"

"He can't keep me grounded forever. Is Wynona going, or is she still too embarrassed and afraid she'll run into the cute blonde lifeguard she had a crush on?" Maddie grinned, remembering the look on Wynona's face when she tossed a pillow at Val and fell off the sofa.

Val faked a gag. "The way she whines, I'm not sure I want her there, but I guess I should ask. She'll never let me forget it if I don't invite her. I hope Cal will let you come."

"I won't see him until Saturday, but Momma can ask him for me." She tossed in her books and spun the tumbler on the combination lock to secure it. "I'll let you know by Wednesday. Keep your fingers crossed."

***

"Hi, Maddie. How did your day go?" Belva asked when Maddie came home from school.

"It went fine, Momma. Did you remember to ask Cal if I can go to Val's party Friday night?" Maddie tossed her notebook and handbag into Cal's recliner and kicked off her shoes.

"I did." Belva motioned for Maddie to pick up the shoes and books. "I talked to him before he left for work. He said he would have to think it over because you still haven't paid for the boat canvas."

"How can I pay for the canvas? I had to quit my job because he took my car keys for something I didn't do! How does he expect me to pay? With my lunch money?" Maddie slumped onto the sofa with her shoes and books on her lap and pouted.

"He hasn't said you can't go." Belva said. She marveled at how much the fire in Maddie's gray-blue eyes reminded her of Cal's eyes whenever he lost his temper.

"No, he hasn't! He wants to torment me for as long as possible and then say no!"

"I'll talk to him again tomorrow, Maddie. There's still time."

"Don't even bother with it, Momma. I don't care what he says. I should have known better than to ask." She jerked the phone from the end table beside the recliner, stacked it up on top of the rest of her armload, and stomped off down the hall to her room.

***

Maddie called Val to vent her frustrations. "Cal won't tell me whether I can go to the party Friday, but I'm going. Will you pick me up?" She twisted the receiver cord around her finger and paced back and forth until her legs wound-up in the phone extension wire.

"Sure, I can stop by there on my way, but won't you get into even more trouble? I don't want to get in the middle between you and your Dad."

"Oh, he won't mess with you. It's me he despises," Maddie said through clamped jaws and gritted teeth, trying to untangle herself.

"Okay, if you're sure. I'm glad you're going. It wouldn't be as much fun without you, Mads."

***

Frankie called Thursday evening. "I've missed you this week, Maddie, and I'd love to see you tomorrow night. Will you let me take you out for a burger and a movie?"

"I have plans already. There's a pool party at Mountainside Park for the swim team, and I promised Val I would be there. Why don't you come to the party?" She crossed her fingers hoping for a yes.

"Sure, what time should I pick you up?"

"Um–you should just meet me at the park–say, around 7:00?"

"I'll be there," Frankie said. "Should I bring something? Beer? Wine?"

Maddie giggled. "You are old. In case you've forgotten, this is a high school swim party with chaperones. And it's inside the park where no alcoholic beverages are allowed. So no---no beer or wine."

"Thanks for reminding me of my age, kiddo." He groaned and imitated the voice of an old man. "Eh, what'd ye say, missy? Us old folks don't hear so well."

She giggled again. "Bye, Frankie, see ya Friday."

***

Friday evening, Maddie covered her swimsuit with a periwinkle blue tee shirt and cut-off blue jean shorts rolled to mid-thigh. She slipped her feet into her white thong sandals and pulled her hair into a ponytail then checked the mirror. Before leaving her room, she coated her lips with pink lip gloss and dabbed on the Chanel No.5 Belinda had given her for Christmas last year.

"Be back by 11:00," Belva said as Maddie emerged from her room, humming and smiling.

"Val isn't much of a night owl, so we should be back by then." She sat on the sofa beside Belva. "Don't worry, Momma. If Cal gets mad, it won't matter. He stays mad most of the time anyway."

"It's not Cal I'm worried about, Maddie." She laid aside the bird picture she was embroidering onto a white fabric square. "Just be careful, okay?"

"I will, Momma." Maddie wondered if Belva somehow sensed that she was not being honest, but pushed the thought aside when Val honked the horn in the driveway. "I'll try to be back by eleven, but I'll have to wait for Val to bring me home."

***

Frankie drove his Mini Cooper into Mountainside Park and circled the lot, looking for the best parking space. He backed into the spot nearest the exit and raised the convertible top before pulling his towel from the back seat, then set off to find Maddie.

Wynona met him at the pool entrance and wasted no time dragging him into the midst of the other party guests. She complimented his choice of a snug-fitting, red Ralph Lauren polo shirt, L.L. Bean khaki shorts, and black Birkenstock sandals that emphasized both his toned physique and his financial status. She slipped her arm through his and introduced him as if he were her date.

Maddie and Val rounded the curve in the pebbled walkway leading from the parking lot to the pool. "I wonder what's going on over there?" Val pointed to a huddle of folks near the pool entrance. "Whatever it is, it must be fun. Everyone is laughing."

"Let's go see," Maddie said. They dropped their lawn chairs in the shade of the pool house and strolled toward the group. Ten paces away, Maddie heard Wynona laughing louder than the others. The closer she came to the group, the more curious she grew. "Is that Frankie's voice?"

Val edged herself into the huddle to get a peek at the entertainment. "That is Frankie, and Wynona is hanging all over him!"

Maddie eased into the group behind Val and her jaw dropped. Wynona was pressing her chest into Frankie's back and rubbing her hands over his shoulders and biceps while laughing at his corny one-liner jokes. Frankie, without doubt, was relishing her affections. The crowd dwindled, but Maddie and Val waited for the love-birds to acknowledge them.

"Come on over, ladies," Frankie said when he noticed them. "We've been having a great time waiting for you." He motioned them closer.

Val stepped forward, assumed a protective stance between Maddie and Frankie, and eyed them with the scrutiny of a tiger protecting her cubs. "I can see you and Wynona are enjoying each other well enough. I've never seen her so—carefree." She beamed Wynona an *I will make your life miserable* stare.

"I introduced Frankie to the crowd." Wynona snuggled into him. "Everybody loves him, but why shouldn't they? He's the friendliest and most handsome man in the park."

Maddie's jaws clenched and her face tightened. "What's the matter, Maddie?" Wynona walked her fingers across the back of Frankie's neck. "Not jealous are you?"

Frankie pushed her hands away and patted her on the shoulder then went to Maddie. "Are you okay, Maddie?"

"Yes, Frankie, I'm fine. Wynona is the one who is not herself," she said, still glaring at Wynona.

"I couldn't help but notice she's somewhat inebriated." Frankie pretended to sip from a bottle.

"She's drunk? Wynona is drunk? Oh—my—word!" Maddie went to the rock wall surrounding the pool where Wynona sat swaying and giggling. "What are you doing, Wynona?" She leaned close and whispered. "You know alcohol isn't allowed in the park. If the rangers find out you're drinking, they will throw you out."

Wynona raised her hands high above her head as she swayed. In a not-so-quiet, sing-song way she said, "I'm shedding the anxiety and living without care." Then she whispered, "The park rangers won't be joining our party, so they'll never know if you don't tell them." She shoved Maddie away with her crutch and hobbled her way toward the pool. Halfway there, she looked back over her shoulder at Frankie. "Come and find me later, handsome. If Maddie is not woman enough for you tonight, I'll be happy to oblige."

Maddie felt the blood rush to her face and her jaws clench.

"She'll be all right Maddie," Frankie said. "She'll be puking her guts out before the party is over. When she wakes up tomorrow morning with a hangover, she'll be sorry and embarrassed by her behavior. Let's go have fun. Race you to the pool."

Maddie hesitated, then dismissed Wynona's drunken immorality. No need to ruin Val's celebration. She shrugged away the implications of what she'd just witnessed, kicked off her sandals, and stripped to her bikini as she ran. When Frankie didn't follow, she looked back to find him standing in the same spot where she had left him, gazing at her.

"Aren't you coming to the pool? It's not a race if you're not running."

He trotted to her side and put his arm around her waist. "You are stunning in that bikini. I had to catch my breath."

Maddie pulled her towel to her chest when she realized he was still ogling her. "Stop that! You're embarrassing me."

Frankie grinned and ticked his eyebrows in his usual playful manner. "I couldn't help myself. I promise I won't do it again, unless you're not looking,"

They spent the next hour splashing and flirting until someone called, "Burgers are ready! Come and get it!" Maddie tied her towel around her waist, and they walked arm in arm to the grill.

"Has anyone seen Wynona since she made her debut?" Val asked, loud enough for the crowd to hear.

"Not since a half-hour ago," Maddie said. "She was over on the landing out past the diving board with a group of boys. Why do you ask?"

"I hope she didn't get arrested for public drunkenness." The disgust pasted all over Val's face didn't override the concerned tone of her voice.

"We'll go look for her." Frankie took Maddie's empty plate and dumped their trash into the garbage container. "Come on. Let's wander around and see if we can find her."

They strolled over the grounds, holding hands and searching the crowd. The warm, gentle evening breeze rustled the blooms on dogwoods and redbuds and filled the air with the scent of late spring, while the faint song of a whippoorwill serenaded them in the moonlight. Frankie squeezed her fingers and leaned close, rubbing his shoulder against hers. "This is nice," he whispered.

"It would be much nicer if we knew where Wynona is." Maddie took a deep breath and let it out in a slow steady exhale. "I hope she's all right."

"Shouldn't we tell someone she's missing?" Frankie asked after they had covered the entire pool and playground areas. "No one seems to have seen her since she left the landing, and the water is not a good place for someone who's tipsy. Maybe we should have the lifeguards drag the pool."

"I can't bear to even think about that, Frankie. Surely if she was in trouble in the water, someone would have noticed, as crowded as it is. Let's give it a few more minutes and check the storage room behind the bathhouse. That's where the lifeguards take their dates when they're on break. Wynona had a crush on the blonde one. In her condition, as I'm sure you know, if she saw him she wouldn't hesitate to show him." A tinge of anger surfaced as she spoke. "I hope she hasn't done something she'll regret."

Frankie knocked on the door of the tiny room. It creaked when he pushed it open. A nuance of light from the lamp on the pool house wall peeked through the port-hole sized window, highlighting the cobwebs draped in the corner. A musty odor curled out of the clammy cubicle into his nostrils. "There's nothing in here but a cot, an old army blanket, and a mass of cobwebs. I doubt anyone has been in here for quite some time."

"There's one other place we should look." Maddie said. She walked toward a row of cedar trees growing a few yards behind the bath house.

"You seem to know your way around this place. You must have history here."

"Yeah, when you grow up around here you get to know the park, and I worked here last summer."

"Then lead me on," Frankie said and reached for her hand.

Maddie went out in front and Frankie followed her down a little pig trail leading into the woods. A tiny, rustic duplex cabin stood a few yards ahead in the clearing. Two doors with two sets of pine plank risers and two rollout windows comprised the entire front. A dim light glowed through the window in unit two, suggesting someone was there.

Frankie knocked. "Hello, anybody in there?" He shielded his eyes with his hands and peeked through the glass. He knocked again, this time on the window pane.

"Go away. This is a private cabin," a youthful male voice called back.

Frankie knocked louder this time and bare feet padded toward the door. The door swung wide and a tall, muscular, blonde teenager stood in the doorway in his underpants, looking perturbed and smelling of beer. "Who are you and what do you want?" He frowned his displeasure at the disruption.

"I'm sorry to disturb you," Frankie said. "We're looking for Wynona Wade, and we thought she might be here. She's five-foot two, blondish, and wearing a cast on her ankle. Have you seen her?"

"Who wants to know? You're not her brother, are you?" The lifeguard ran his fingers through his blonde curls and narrowed the opening in the doorway.

"No, she's an acquaintance of mine and a pal of my friend Maddie here. So have you seen her?"

He opened the door wider and stepped aside. "Come on in. She's passed out on the bed. We're not supposed to have girls in the cabin, and the rangers drop in at random. I need her out of here. Maybe you can wake her up."

Maddie breathed a sigh of relief. "Thank God!" She said.

Wynona lay sprawled on her stomach across the lifeguard's cot, limp and lifeless. Maddie rolled her over and checked her breathing. "She's out cold. We need to call her parents to come and get her. Is there a phone in this cabin?"

"Hold up a moment," Frankie said. "Let's take her outside into the fresh air and try to sober her up first. Is there any coffee in this cabin?" He turned to the lifeguard. "You, what's your name?"

"Eddie, but everyone calls me Beau. There's instant coffee in the pantry. I'll heat the water."

Frankie lifted Wynona off the bed, carried her outside and put her on the ground on Maddie's beach towel. Maddie soaked a wash cloth in cool water and swabbed her face and neck for several minutes until she blinked and her eyes rolled back. When Frankie lifted her to sitting position, she opened her eyes. Her words slurred when she spoke. "Hi, Maddie. What are you doing here?"

"I'm here to sober you up and take you home. You're drunk!"

"Where is that coffee, Beau?" Frankie called into the cabin.

"I have it," he said, and handed the cup through the door to Frankie.

Frankie held the cup to her lips. "Take a sip, Wynona." She sniffed his shirt.

"Frankie, you smell good," she said, then leaned forward and vomited on his feet.

"I don't now." Frankie shook the smelly up-chuck off his sandals.

Forty-five minutes and three cups of coffee later, Wynona could stand without support. Frankie pitched his car keys to Maddie and said, "I'll drive her home in her car. You can follow me in mine. Can you drive a stick shift?"

She caught the keys with both hands. "Yeah, my Carmen Ghia is a stick shift. I'll go back to the pool and tell Val we're leaving, then I'll meet you in the parking lot."

Wynona's mother flipped on the light and walked out on the front porch when Maddie knocked. "Wynona wasn't able to drive, Mrs. Wade, so we brought her home. She's not feeling well."

Mrs. Wade's face set in a hardened expression. "She's not sick, she's drunk. I've seen enough drunks to know the difference. Her grandpa was a drunk, her daddy is a drunk, and it looks as if Wynona will be just like them. I wanted better for her." The corners of Mrs. Wade's lips upturned slightly, but her attempted smile didn't hide the anguish her eyes. "Thank you for bringing her home, Maddie. Good night."

She led Wynona inside, shut the door behind her, and turned off the porch light. Maddie looked at Frankie and tears puddled in her eyes. "I never knew," she said.

"Let's go Maddie. I'll take you home."

CHAPTER 13

"I don't want to go home yet, Frankie. Momma is not expecting me until 11:00, and it's only 10:15. Could we drive around for a while?" Maddie asked as they neared her driveway.

"Sure, if that's what you want." He drove past her driveway and pulled in at Burke Elementary School, not stopping until the car was out of sight from the road. "I don't want Aunt Ruby to snitch on you," he said.

He walked around the car and opened the passenger door for Maddie to get out. He slipped his arms around her waist and lifted her onto the hood. "How did you become so sweet in so few years, Maddie Randall?" He pressed himself against her knees, leaned in and kissed away the tears on the cheek.

"Don't cry, Maddie," he whispered, as he walked his fingers up her spine and fondled her neck. She dropped her defenses and succumbed to the tenderness of his embrace. Crickets chirped their night time love melodies in perfect synchrony while the pine-sated evening air drifted into her nostrils. Her resolve melted, her knees weakened. His hands reached for forbidden places. Sweet surrender beckoned. *Come in to my vineyard and taste my wine, my garden of delight. Fulfill your desires in my haven and soar to heights only I can give* . . .

A horn toot from a car on Burke Road shattered the enchanted globe and dispelled sin's shrewdly crafted illusion. Maddie wrenched from his grip and squinted at her wristwatch. "I have to go, Frankie. I'm late. We shouldn't have done this."

He reached for her, but she backed away with her raised hands, palms pressing outward as if pushing away air.

Her voice trembled when she spoke again. "I'm sorry, I should have stopped you."

"You have nothing to be sorry for, Maddie."

She straightened her clothing and opened the car door to get in. "I need to go now."

The sounds of their synchronized breathing filled the empty silence on the short drive from Burke Elementary to her driveway.

Cal's headlights beamed through the back window of Frankie's car, and Maddie's pounding heart raced. "He's home from work early," Maddie said, fumbling for the door handle. "You should go now."

Cal waited for Maddie to get out of the car then approached the Mini-Cooper on the driver's side. She couldn't see his face in the darkness, but his heavy footsteps and in-charge swagger conveyed what she dreaded. He was angry.

Frankie opened his car door and offered Cal his hand. "I'm Frankie Mason."

Cal ignored the gesture. "Who gave you permission to be out with my daughter?"

"But Daddy, he drove me home from the park." Maddie said, hoping to forego an embarrassing scene.

"Get in the house, Maddie, now!" The stern, pragmatic tone dared her to disobey.

Belva turned on the porch light and met her at the door. Cal and Frankie talked in matter-of-fact tones, but neither raised his voice. Then, without commotion, Frankie left and Cal stomped into the living room. He slammed the door so hard the window rattled.

"Where were you, young lady?" Cal asked Maddie, but cast an angry glare toward Belva. "Is this how your mother lets you behave when I'm not here?"

She kept her eyes glued to Belva. "I went to a cookout with Val, but Frankie drove me home because I promised Momma I'd be home early."

He gestured toward her room. "Go to bed. We'll settle this tomorrow."

Maddie got into bed, but she couldn't sleep. She turned her head to the wall and pulled the pillow over her ears to muffle the sound of Cal brow-beating Belva. *What have I done?*

***

Saturday morning, Maddie woke with a headache and a crick in her neck. She rolled her head from side to side to relieve the tightness and yelped from the pain. Belva knocked on the wall outside her room. "May I come in?"

"Yes, Momma."

Belva lifted the privacy curtain and stepped into the room. "Are you all right, Maddie?"

"Yeah, there's a crick in my neck and my head hurts, but I'm fine." She twisted her head and rubbed her neck.

"I didn't mean that. I mean from last night. Who was that who drove you home, and why was Cal talking to him for so long?" She sat at the foot of the bed and waited while Maddie fluffed her pillows and stuffed them behind her back.

"That was Frankie Mason, Momma. I met him at St. John's when I worked there, and I invited him to Val's celebration party."

"Oh, Maddie, I wish you had let me meet him before you went out with him."

"I didn't let you meet him because he's older than me, and I figured Cal wouldn't let me go out with him if he knew."

The throb in Maddie's head intensified from the burn of Belva's disappointed eyes. She broke eye contact with her Momma. "Is there any coffee left from breakfast?"

"No, but let's go make another pot. I could use a second cup."

"Is Cal up this morning?" Maddie asked, while Belva filled the coffee pot with water.

"He's up, but he's out in the shed putting the new canvas cover on the pontoon boat. He hasn't mentioned last night."

Maddie didn't want to talk about last night's confrontation. "Wynona was drinking last night. I didn't believe she would do that, but she was so drunk Frankie and I had to take her home. When we dropped her off, Mrs. Wade told us that Mr. Wade is an alcoholic, and so was his dad."

Belva didn't speak but sat down at the table in the chair next to Maddie.

"Wynona never talked about her family life, so I didn't know. Why wouldn't she tell me when we're supposed to be friends?"

"You mean like the way you didn't tell me about Frankie?"

The *blurp, blurp, blurp* of the percolator reverberated in Maddie's head, and the stink of betrayal overpowered the coveted aroma of the brewing coffee.

"I didn't mean to hurt you, Momma."

"I'm sure you didn't mean to, Maddie, but I trusted you, and you've lied to me twice."

Maddie shoved her fingers through her hair and held her head in her hands with her elbows propped on the table. Sorrowful sobs erupted from her. When her shoulders stopped quaking, she pulled a paper napkin from the plastic holder on the table and dabbed her red eyes and watery nose. "I'm—worse—than—Cal," she said, between sniffles. "I love you, Momma, and I'm sorry I lied. Will you forgive me?"

Belva moved her chair closer and enveloped Maddie's hands in hers. "I'll forgive you, Maddie, because I love you. But forgiveness doesn't mean there won't be consequences." She squeezed Maddie's hands, then rose from her chair and poured two mugs of coffee.

"I'll pray about it and we'll see. In the meantime, you should pray for yourself. You need the Father's forgiveness more than you need mine."

***

Cal didn't come inside until late in the afternoon. "Bring me some cold water, Belva. It must be ninety-five degrees out there in that shed."

He watched Maddie moving around in the living room where she was watching TV and talking on the phone. The receiver clacked when she placed it back in the cradle. "Come in here, Maddie."

Her pulse quickened. "I'm coming," she said, then braced herself for a tongue lashing. She straightened her shoulders, walked into the kitchen, and waited for him to pounce. Instead, he eyed her up and down as if he were inspecting her, making her feel even more uncomfortable. After staring at her face, chest, and hips for several seconds, he spoke, but not in his usual tone. He spoke to her for the first time as if she were a mature adult.

"The next time you find a new boyfriend I'd like to meet him before he takes you out. What do you know about him? How old is he?"

"Frankie is twenty-four. He's studying to be a doctor."

"He's not a boy, he's a man. And a man his age who dates teenaged girls is not looking for a wife. I expect you to behave yourself from here on out. If you want to be treated as an adult, it's time you learned to behave like one."

Maddie didn't respond, but waited for a harsh outburst. He reached into his shirt pocket and pulled out her key ring. "Here are your car keys. How much money do you have?"

What is he up to? she thought, then answered. "I saved seventy-two dollars from my job, and I have thirty-eight dollars more that I withdrew from my savings account."

Without further banter, he said, "Give me the seventy-two dollars, and we'll call it even on the canvas. I needed a new one anyway, so I'll pay the other half."

"Okay, I'll get it." She hurried to her room, pulled the envelope from her coat pocket, and counted it to be sure, then hurried back to the kitchen before he changed his mind. She handed Cal her money, still wary of his motives.

"Come here and give your old daddy a hug," Cal said, and stretched his arms toward her with a satisfied grin on his face.

Taken aback and not knowing what else to do, she hugged him and said, "Thank you." She strode back to the living room unsure of what had just happened, but relieved.

Sunday morning came, and Maddie readied herself for church without Belva reminding her. She took the remaining cash from her wallet and counted out eight dollars. When the usher passed the plate during the church service, she dropped it in with a happy heart. Belva smiled.

During the prayer, Maddie thanked God for her car and for Cal relieving half her debt. "It had to be You, because it was a miracle." She understood that to repent meant to turn away from wrong, so she never confessed her behavior with Frankie.

Chapter 14

When Wynona didn't show up for their usual Monday morning locker social, Val and Maddie worried. "Did you know her dad and granddad are alcoholics?" Maddie asked.

"No, but if I had known she had such a bad home life, I might have been more forgiving of her attitude. But, who knows? She might still be a pain even without family troubles."

Maddie laughed., "You may be right, Val."

***

At noon, Wynona slipped into the cafeteria line behind Maddie and Val. "Hey girls, did you miss me this morning?"

"Wy, you're here, and you're not wearing your cast. Why didn't you tell us you were getting it taken off today?"

"You didn't ask," she said, then joined in with her usual snappy comebacks.

No one mentioned Friday night until after school as the girls chatted in the parking lot. "Want a ride home, Wynona?" Maddie asked.

"You got your car back? Did Frankie give you the money to pay off your debt?"

"Nobody gave me any money, Wynona. I don't know what happened. Cal did the most unusual thing Saturday morning. He gave me back my keys and told me he would settle for half the cost of the canvas."

"Lucky you. My mom gave me a two-hour lecture on Saturday morning while I still had a hangover. She wouldn't even let me drink any coffee."

Maddie reached across the seat and unlocked the passenger side door of her VW. "She's worried that you'll become an alcoholic. Why didn't you tell me about your dad and your grandpa, Wynona?"

Wynona sat down in the passenger seat and closed the door. "Because I thought you wouldn't understand. Cal gives you a hard time, but nothing like my dad does to mom and me. When he comes home drunk, he slaps Mom around and sometimes he . . . Never mind." She turned her face away and stared out the window.

Curious about what could be more humiliating than Cal's belittlement, Maddie probed. "What does he do Wynona? I promise I won't judge."

Wynona fidgeted with the zipper-pull on her denim jacket. "He comes into my room at night, and I can't make him stop." A tear formed in her eye but she wiped it way with her sleeve before it could fall. "I can't tell Mom. I'm afraid she would kill him. Then she'd go to jail, and I'd be alone. You can't ever tell anyone I told you, Maddie."

"You mean he gets into your bed? Wy, you have to tell your mother, or the authorities, or someone who can stop him." Maddie reached across the stick-shift to hold Wynona's hand, but she jerked it away.

"No! No one would believe me, and if they did, they wouldn't treat me the same. It's horrible enough without people knowing it. I'm sorry for the way I behaved with Frankie on Friday night." Her mouth curved into a weak smile.

Embarrassed by her own naivety, and not knowing what else to say, Maddie asked, "Why do you drink, Wynona? Can't you see what it's done to your dad? Aren't you afraid it will happen to you too?"

"Sometimes, but I do it anyway. When I'm drunk, I can forget what he does. I'm getting out of there as soon as I turn eighteen and get a job."

"You need to get out of there now and stop drinking before it wrecks your life and you end up just like him." Maddie started the engine and pushed the gearstick into reverse. Wynona opened the door and got out.

"Thanks for offering me a ride home, but I'll ride the bus."

"Wait, Wynona. I didn't mean …"

She was already boarding the bus before Maddie could stop her.

***

At home, Maddie debated whether she should call Frankie. They had neared a point of no return, and she didn't want him to think she wanted to do that again. Yet she was curious to know what he and Cal had said to each other. Whatever it was, it satisfied Cal, because he hadn't picked on her this week. And then there was that strange incident where he had given her keys back. She ditched the thought and called Wynona instead.

"Hello, Wynona. I'm sorry if I pushed you too hard. I hope you're not still mad at me."

An awkward silence lingered a moment before she answered. "I'm not mad at you, Maddie. There's nothing I can do to fix it, so there's no need to talk about it."

"I understand," Maddie said. "I won't bring it up again."

Another moment of silence, then a titter of laughter from Wynona lightened the air. "Tell me how big a fool I made of myself Friday evening."

"How did you end up in the lifeguard's hut?" Maddie laughed, glad the tension had lifted.

"I was so drunk, I don't remember! First Beau sees me in a stinky mess after the storm, and now he sees me as a drunken mess. I guess I can say

I 'messed' up my chances with him." She laughed again then asked, "Maddie, do you think God would help me if I went to church?"

Surprised by Wynona's interest she said, "Well, there's a spiritual peace that comes with being in church. It helps me whenever I'm confused. But it's not just church. It's the relationship with God that does it."

"I have no relationship with God, Maddie. I guess he doesn't want a drunk for a child."

"Don't be ridiculous, Wynona. God loves you. Why don't you ask Him?"

"Yeah, maybe I will." Maddie thought she caught the sound of a sniffle, then Wynona faked a cough. I think I'm coming down with something. I'll talk to you later."

"Bye, Wynona."

Maddie went outside to the front porch and sat in the oversized, cane bottomed rocking chair that had once belonged to Granny Nettie. Surrounded by the wide arms and towering back, she felt small and safe. She closed her eyes and rocked, listening to the sound of crickets chirping and frogs croaking in Uncle Josh's pond.

"Abba, are you here with me? Wynona needs your help, but she won't ask. Will you help her anyway? Please put a want in her heart to come to you. And, about Frankie, Lord, I'm weak and I'm scared. Even though I'm not in love with him, the strong attraction between us is more than I can resist. Why do I do the wrong thing when I know what's right? Please forgive me for what I've done, and strengthen me to say no. Thank you, Abba." She rocked on and hummed her favorite hymn, "Tis So Sweet to Trust in Jesus" until Belva called her in for supper. That night she slept better than she had slept since the day of the storm.

CHAPTER 15

Three weeks passed without a call from Frankie. Then one Friday evening, he showed up in Maddie's driveway. She met him outside before he got out of the car. "I haven't seen you in a while. What brings you out this way?" She stood more than an arm's length away from the driver's side window and never invited him to come in.

"I've been in Memphis getting enrolled in medical school for next term, and I'm back in town for the next two weeks. Do you want to catch a flick at the drive-in tonight?"

"No, I don't—I don't know, Frankie?"

"Is your dad home?"

"No, Momma is here." She took a step closer to the car and stooped to meet his eyes. "What did Cal say to you last time you were here?"

"Not much." He turned down one corner of his mouth and lifted his shoulders in a nonchalant shrug. "I got the impression he didn't want me to see you, but he didn't say I couldn't."

Maddie walked toward the front porch. He got out of the car and followed. "Let's get out of here for a while," he said.

She walked on and watched her feet to avoid looking at him. "Will you come to church with me on Sunday, Frankie?"

"Church? Why?"

"Why not?" she answered.

"I'm not a church goer, Maddie. I doubt if I'll ever be."

"I won't get involved with anyone who doesn't believe, so there's no reason for us to spend time together."

He took two quick steps ahead of her, turned to face her, and placed his hands on her shoulders. "We're not talking about marriage or long term. Let's have a good time. What could be wrong with that? Don't you enjoy my company?"

"I do. I'm not looking for someone to marry either, and the chemistry between us is more than I want right now. You should find someone who wants the same thing you do."

"You're what I want, Maddie." He traced his hand across her cheek, lifted her face, and peered into her eyes. The dimple in his cheek sunk deeper when his smile grew wider.

Maddie's heart fluttered, and a smile sneaked up on her. "I guess we could see a movie."

"Good." Frankie's eyes brightened. *"Gone with the Wind* is playing at the Northside Drive-In."

Maddie slipped her arm through his and said, "I loved the book."

At the theater Frankie parked mid-way between the movie screen and the snack bar and put the top down on the Mini Cooper. The portable speaker crackled with static when he slipped it into the floorboard beneath his feet and adjusted the volume. "Is that loud enough?"

"That's perfect."

Frankie came back from the snack bar with two colas and a huge box of popcorn that looked nothing like the perfectly popped kernels in the advertisements scrolling across the screen They finished their colas and popcorn before the movie started.

When the title and opening credits scrolled, Frankie slouched into his bucket seat and reached for Maddie's hand. She enjoyed the smoothness of his skin as he weaved his fingers through hers.

Halfway through the movie, the screen gave way to more food temptations while they waited for the second reel to start. Frankie straightened himself in his seat. "This little sports car does not make a good theater chair," he said. "Let's get out and stretch for a minute."

"I need to visit the ladies room," she said. She reached into the backseat for her blue macramé purse and started toward the concession stand with Frankie tagging along beside her.

"I'll do the same for the gentlemen's room," he said.

In the restroom she refreshed her lipstick and fluffed her hair before going back out. Frankie met her near the spot where they'd split company, and they headed back toward the car. "Are you enjoying the movie?"

"The book was better, but yes, it's good."

"Since you know the ending, do you mind if we go somewhere? We can't talk while we're watching a movie." He guided her toward the car with his hand at the small of her back.

"Where do you want to go? It's getting late, and I have to be home by eleven."

"I know a place, and I'll have you home on time, I promise."

"Okay, I guess." Maddie hesitated for a moment, then agreed. "But, just to talk."

They left the theater and drove back toward home. A half-mile before they reached Burke Road, Frankie turned off the highway onto what appeared to be a barn road or wagon trail. "My Uncle Ted leases this place. He raises hay and stores it in the big barn on the back side of the fields. He won't mind if we park here."

Maddie toyed with the charms on her bracelet. "This place is spooky."

"I won't let anything get you, Maddie. There's just you and me and a few friendly critters out here. It's safe enough. You'll see." He pulled into the barnyard and got out of the car. "See how peaceful it is?"

Maddie leaned her head back against the headrest and looked up. "It's been a long time since I've sat under the stars and enjoyed the evening sky. It is so majestic."

Frankie pulled a blanket out of the backseat, spread it out on the ground beside the car, and lay on his back gazing toward heaven. He motioned her to the spot beside him.

Maddie got out of the car, kicked off her sandals, and sat on the edge of the blanket, sliding her bare feet through the soft grass. Frankie sat up beside her, put his arm around her back, and nuzzled his face into her neck.

"What are you doing? I thought we came here to talk and enjoy the stars." Maddie pushed him away, but he grabbed her shoulders and pulled her backward as he fell. Before she could get up, he threw his body across her and kissed her with fiery passion. She returned his kiss. As their passion grew, Frankie reached for the bottom of her tee shirt, and she froze.

"I can't do this, Frankie. It's not right. Please take me home."

"Take you home? You lead me on and tease me into believing you want this, and then you say no?"

"Please, take me home."

Frankie unbuckled his belt and slid his pants off with his right hand while pinning her to the blanket with his left arm. His lust-glazed eyes scared her. She struggled to free herself but his strong arms and body held her to the ground. He reached for the button on her jeans. "You want this as much as I do, Maddie. You need to shed your inhibitions and go with it."

She screamed and pushed against him with all her strength, but he didn't budge. He capped his left hand over her mouth, and she dug her teeth into it. He raised his right hand to slap her, but froze mid-air. Then his countenance softened as if he realized what he'd done. He rolled off her and sat up, wiping the blood from his wound. She scrambled to her feet, grabbed her sandals and ran down the dark, weed-covered trail toward Burke Road.

Before she reached the highway, she heard the rumble of the car's engine. She pushed her way through the bushes on the roadside and hid herself behind a large oak tree. Her breath came in labored gasps and her heartbeats sounded like thunder in her head. She prayed he wouldn't come looking for her.

Frankie eased his Mini Cooper down the barn road, stopping every few feet to call out to her.

"I'm sorry, Maddie. I lost control. I won't do it again. Come on, let me take you home."

She clamped her hand across her mouth to hold in the scream when a field mouse scurried through the leaves near her feet, then parked himself on the top of her foot. "Get off, get off, get off!" Scared to move and scared not to, she sent mental commands to the mouse, who paid her no mind.

"I don't want to leave you out here in the woods by yourself, Maddie. I promise I won't hurt you."

She envisioned the feral pop-eyed glare she had seen gawking down at her when he had her pinned to the ground. *No way, Frankie Mason. I'd rather take my chances out here with the wild animals and snakes than to ever get back into your car again.* When she didn't answer, he revved the engine and sped away. Trembling and afraid, she let out a low moan and shuffled her feet through the leaves at the base of the tree until the mouse raced back into the bushes.

The moonlight reflected against the dial of her wrist watch. Eleven o'clock. A prayer and a hymn escaped her trembling lips, summoning the courage to move her from her temporary refuge. She swiped her face with the back of her hand, dried the tears, and stepped out from behind the tree, still trembling. Ducking behind the bushes and crouching with every noise, she made her way to the highway and ran in the direction of home.

Maddie knocked on the door of a nearby house and the porch light came on. A thin gray haired man pulled back the lacy curtain and peeked out through the glass, then opened the door. "I'm sorry to bother you this late, sir," Maddie said, her voice shaking. "May I please use your telephone?"

The old man stepped out on the porch and noticed her frayed and tattered look. Tears stained her face and black streaks trailed from her melted mascara. "What happened to you, child? Come in, please."

"Thank you, sir. I need to call home."

"Come here, Mom." He motioned to his wife who sat in a rocking chair with a ball of yarn and a crochet hook. "This young lady needs a woman's touch. You take care of her and I'll get her a glass of water."

The elderly woman struggled to raise herself from the chair and laid her crochet project in a basket at her feet. She hobbled over to Maddie and led her by the elbow to a spot on the end of an afghan-covered sofa. "Poor child, whatever is a pretty girl like you doing out alone at night? Sit here and rest until John gets back with your water." She patted Maddie's hand with motherly affection.

The old man handed Maddie a class of water. She swallowed a sip and set the glass on the end table, then dialed the number for home. It rang several times before Belva answered.

"Momma?" Maddie broke into tears.

"Is that you, Maddie? What's wrong? Where are you?" Maddie felt Belva's panic through the phone.

"I'm all right, Momma. I need someone to pick me up. Is Daddy home?"

"No, honey. He's not home from work yet. Where are you?"

"I'm on Burke Road, not far from the main highway." She mustered a smile at the elderly couple. "A nice man and his wife let me use their phone. Will you send someone to come and get me?"

"I'll call Belinda and Jim. What's the address?"

Maddie stood by the door watching for Jim's car.

"What is your name, child?" The old man asked.

"I'm Maddie Randall."

"Do you know Cal Randall?" Though standing next to her, his voice sounded distant to Maddie.

135

"Yes, I'm his daughter. How do you know Cal?"

"I worked with him at the White Stores back in the early fifties. I'm John, and this is my wife Georgia. Is he still in this part of the country? Someone told me he moved to California."

She tried to be cordial, but she didn't want to talk about Cal or California. She wanted to go home. With her eyes peeled to the road, watching for approaching headlights, she said, "Yes, he did, twice." Before John could ask his next question, Jim's headlights beamed in the driveway. "My ride is here, sir. Thank you for the water and the phone call." The old man caught the screen door before it banged against the wall as Maddie rushed through it.

Chapter 16

"Who did this to you, Sis?" Belinda braced herself against Jim's pickup truck to counter the force from her sister's clinging hug.

Jim butted in. "Who is he, Maddie? He's not getting away with this!"

Maddie shuddered and buried her face deeper into Belinda's shoulder.

"Hush up, Jim. Can't you see you're making it worse? Tell us what happened, Maddie."

"It's my fault. I should have known better than to leave the movie before time to go home. He's been so nice I never believed he would hurt me."

"How did he hurt you, Maddie?" Belinda pulled loose from her grasp and looked her up and down.

"He didn't, but only because I ran away. He held me down, so I couldn't move. I was so scared. I bit him and grabbed my shoes and ran." Maddie sniffled. "I'm sorry you had to come and get me."

Belva stopped pacing when Jim's car rolled into the gravel driveway. "Oh, Maddie, are you okay?" she asked when Maddie stepped out of the car into her outstretched arms. "What happened? Where is Frankie?"

"I don't know where he is, and I never want to see him again! He tried to rape me!"

Jim spun the car around in the yard and sped out of the driveway slinging gravels behind him. "I hope he doesn't find him tonight," Belinda said.

In the kitchen, Belva warmed a wet wash cloth and swabbed Maddie's forehead and face. "Are you hurt, Sweetie? We'll take you to the hospital and let them check."

"No. I'm all right, just scared." Maddie said, then laughed through her tears. "I can't say the same for him though. I bit a hunk out of his hand."

"Good for you, Sis. I hope he gets rabies. That'll teach him to mess with Mad-Dog Maddie." Belinda snarled and growled. They were still laughing when Cal came through the door.

"What's so funny? Why are you here this late, Belinda? What's going on?"

The room quietened and their faces grew solemn. "Frankie Mason tried to rape Maddie. Jim has gone to find him."

Cal turned and stomped out of the room. A few minutes later, he came back with his pistol and a box of ammo. "What are you doing Cal? Put that gun away!" Belva grasped his shirt sleeve as he swarmed by her. He jerked loose and hustled through the back door and left. He raced out of the driveway with greater fury than Jim.

***

Belva and Belinda met Cal and Jim at the back door at 2:15 a.m. when they returned. "Did you find him?" They both asked at the same time.

"No, but this ain't over," Jim said. "We'll file a complaint against him tomorrow morning. He's not getting away with this."

"Please just let it go," Maddie pleaded. "He didn't hurt me, and I don't want everyone to know. I'm so embarrassed. Please don't."

"Go to bed and rest, Maddie." Belinda said. "Let's go home, Jim. We can come back in the morning when everyone has slept."

"Okay," Jim said. "But I will be back in the morning, Cal. We'll find him."

Belva followed them to the door and locked up for the night. In Maddie's room, she bent to kiss her daughter on the forehead and tucked the blankets in around her. "Good night, sweetheart. I'm happy you're safe. Try to sleep."

Maddie lay awake. Every time she closed her eyes, she felt the burn of Frankie's impassioned eyes boring into her. If she had just said no when he wanted to leave the drive-in early, if she hadn't let him touch her, this would not have happened. Why did he do this? Why was he different tonight? What-ifs and whys---questions with no answers---plagued her until her body surrendered to exhaustion. She fell asleep at daybreak, curled around her pillow. Maddie awoke at 11:00 a.m. to the sound of muffled voices in the living room. She slipped her robe on over her pajamas and padded down the hall to find Belinda and Belva sitting on the sofa, looking troubled. "What's going on? Where are Cal and Jim?"

"Good morning, Sis. Come and sit with us." Belinda patted the sofa cushion next to her. "Daddy and Jim went to the sheriff's office this morning to file a complaint against Frankie."

"No! I asked them not to do that!" She burst into tears as Belva tried to console her.

"You didn't let me finish, Maddie," Belinda said. "There's more."

"More? What?"

"When they got to the sheriff's office, a wrecker pulled into the parking lot with a red Mini Cooper in tow. Cal said it was Frankie's. It's messed up bad."

Despite the anger that still boiled in her, she felt the blood drain from her face in dread. "What about Frankie? Did anyone know anything about the accident? How is he? Please, I have to know!"

Belinda squeezed both of Maddie's hands. "The sheriff said the first responders called for the life rescue chopper. They airlifted him to St. John's

Medical Center early this morning, around three o'clock. They wouldn't tell us anything else."

"Oh, no!" Maddie cried out in anguish, and no amount of consolation eased the pain.

***

Once the shock waned, Belinda convinced Maddie to take a nighttime sleep aid she had found in Cal's medicine cabinet. "This is an over-the-counter item, so it's safe," she said, and handed it to Maddie with a glass of water. "Lie down on the sofa, and I'll get you a blanket."

Maddie hid her face in the sofa cushion and sobbed until the sleep aid and the warmth of the blanket helped her fall asleep. She slept until Belva called her to supper.

"You need to eat something, Maddie. You've slept all day." She handed Maddie a damp wash cloth. "Here, wipe your face and hands. I made soup."

"Thank you, Momma, but I'm not hungry."

"I know, Sweetie. But you have to eat." Belva reached for a snack tray and pulled it around in front of Maddie. "Be careful not to spill it. It's steamy hot."

"I need to call St. John's and ask about Frankie. Have you heard any more news?" She looked toward the phone on the end table.

"I called the hospital an hour ago, but they're not giving any information."

"Maybe the nurses I worked with at St. John's can check on him for us. Would you pass me the phone, Momma?"

"I will, but after you've had your soup."

Maddie sipped a few spoonsful of chicken broth and ate two crackers. "That's all I can eat right now. I will try to eat later."

Belva took the tray, handed her the phone, and reached for the telephone directory. "I'll find the number for you."

The phone rang five times, then a male voice answered, "Fourth floor nurse's station. How may I help you?"

Maddie didn't recognize the voice, so she asked to speak to the nurse on duty. "Nurse Connie is with a patient. I'm Paul, today's orderly."

"I'm Maddie Randall, a friend of Frankie Mason. I can't get any word on Frankie's condition. Does anyone on the floor know how he is?"

"He's in critical care. I can walk down to the family waiting room and see if I can pick up any information. Since you and Frankie are friends, I'm sure he won't mind if you check on him."

"Thank you, Paul. Will you call me back soon?"

"Sure," Paul said. "Give me your number."

"Paul is getting information on Frankie's condition," she said to Belva as she hung up the phone. "He said he would call me back later. Will you pray for Frankie, Momma? I want to, but I don't think I can. I'm so confused."

CHAPTER 17

"Thank God, you're not hurt!" Val said when Maddie picked up the phone. "I heard about Frankie's wreck. I'm sooo glad you weren't with him."

"Me too, Val. How did you find out?"

"My dad. He has a CB radio. A truck driver saw it happen. He said Frankie had been tailgating him for several miles and weaving in and out, then passed him in a curve and lost control. The car went airborne and struck a power pole fifteen feet off the ground."

Maddie gasped. "What else did the truck driver say?"

"Dad said the trucker found a bottle of pills on the ground next to the crash site and figured Frankie must have been doped up. No one in their right mind would have tried to pass on that deep curve."

Maddie shuddered. "That explains why he behaved the way he did after we left the drive-in."

"What do you mean?"

"We went to the movies. At the half-time break we went to the restrooms, and then Frankie wanted to leave so we could find a place to talk. He was fine until we got almost home, then we drove out into his uncle's hayfield and parked. Before I knew what was happening, we were on a blanket with him on top of me, and when I told him to stop he didn't. His eyes looked like a hungry wild animal. It was awful, Val."

She sensed tension is Val's voice. "Maddie, are you saying he raped you?"

"No, he stopped when I bit him. When he got off me, I grabbed my shoes and ran. I hid behind a big tree until he gave up looking for me and left. Belinda and Jim had to come and get me."

Val's voice relaxed but sounded sad. "I am so sorry. He seemed like such a nice person. I never dreamed he would do anything like that. Have you told Wynona, Mads?"

"I have told no one except you and my family. I'd rather it be kept quiet. Please don't tell her, Val."

"I feel a little better now, knowing it may have been pills that changed him, and not that he's a rapist," Maddie said.

"Glad I could help."

"I need to hang up now. I'm waiting for a phone call from someone at St. John's about Frankie's condition."

"Call me later if you need to talk. Okay, Mads?"

"I will, Val. Thanks."

The phone rang as soon as Maddie hung up. "This is Paul."

"Great! Do you have any news? What did you find out?"

"Frankie hasn't come around yet from the four surgeries. From what I could gather from bits and pieces of conversations in the waiting room, his nose and cheek bones are smashed. His back is broken in two or three places, both legs are messed up, and he has internal bleeding. The doctor came out to talk to the family while I was still in the waiting room, but he took them into a private room, so I couldn't hear. I tried to read their lips, and it looked like he said *paralyzed*. I can't be sure."

Maddie's head spun. She sat on Cal's recliner and dropped her head to her feet until it eased. Paul was still chattering on the line.

"Are you still there, Maddie? Hello?"

With her head still between her knees, she said, "I'm still here, Paul. You're kind to do this. Thank you for spying for me."

"Espionage is my game. James Bond is my name. I will await your call for my next mission, Madame Randall."

Maddie giggled. "You're funny, Paul."

She hung up the phone and lay back on the sofa. **Why did you do this, Frankie?**

***

Sunday morning at church, the preacher read from Psalms 23 (NKJV)

1.The Lord is my shepherd; I shall not want 2. He makes me to lie down in green pastures; he leads me beside the still waters. 3. He restores my soul.

She thought how majestic the sky had been when she and Frankie were in the field. Before, she had been fearful of the spookiness of the place, but under the stars her fears had vanished until Frankie had lost control and attacked her.

"I need your peace, Abba. Please tell me you are still with me." She whispered a prayer while the preacher talked. Today he didn't pace back and forth and preach hard. The whole church service was serene and calming. She sang along with the hymns of praise and let the message within each of them sink to the depths of her soul. Today Abba spoke to her in hymns and scriptures. He had led her beside still waters and refreshed her soul. "Thank you, Abba."

***

By Monday, Wynona had heard the news. She ran to meet Maddie when she pulled into the student parking lot. "Is Frankie paralyzed? Will he ever walk again, Maddie?"

"I don't know, Wynona. No one can see him except immediate family, and they're keeping quiet."

"Who is his family? Is he related to City Councilman Mason?"

"I don't know," Maddie said. "Frankie never talked about them. I wish I had met them before this happened. Maybe it would help me understand why he did this."

Wynona cocked her head to the side and asked, "Why he did what? I thought he had a car accident from driving too fast. Are you saying there's more to it than that?"

Maddie realized she'd said too much and tried to sway the conversation. "I meant, I wonder if he had family problems."

"I guess everybody has those," Wynona said.

Maddie changed the topic. "What are you doing after school today, Wynona?"

With a half-shrug, Wynona said, "Nothing special. Why?"

"I'm going over to St. John's. Do you want to go with me?" They walked toward the school building as they talked.

"I can do that. But I thought you said Frankie couldn't have visitors?"

"He can't," Maddie said. "I'm planning to skip sixth period study hall so I can go over there and still be home at my usual time. I'd prefer that

Momma and Cal not know. Can you get out of your sixth period class?"

"Sure, I have gym class and our teacher is out today. The substitute won't miss me. What else are you planning, Maddie?"

She ignored her question and said, "Great! I'll meet you at my car after fifth period. I'll ask Val to come along too, when I see her at lunch."

"Well, okay, if you must." Wynona wrinkled her nose and curled her lip to register her disapproval.

Chapter 18

Maddie, Val, and Wynona stepped off the elevator at 3:00 p.m. and asked the receptionist for directions to the CCU waiting room.

"It's around the corner and down the hall just after you pass the water cooler on your right."

"Thank you," Maddie said. The three girls followed the receptionist's directions and came upon double swinging doors with a sign. "Authorized Visitors and Hospital Staff Only." On the wall by the doors hung a buzzer and another sign: "Please Enter Access Code".

"We'll never be allowed in there since we are neither authorized nor staff. Let's come back later when he's out of critical care," Val said.

"Suppose he doesn't come out? I need to see him today," Maddie insisted. "Let's go to the fourth floor and find out if James Bond is on duty. I bet he can show us how to bypass the rules."

"James Bond?" Val questioned. "Who is James Bond?"

Maddie led them down the hall to the elevator. "He's the one who pilfered information on Frankie's condition by eavesdropping in the waiting lounge. The James Bond thing is a joke between the two of us. I've never met him in person, but his name is Paul. I hope he's here today."

On the fourth floor, the three girls stopped at the nurse's station and asked the attendant if they could talk to Paul.

"Sure," the attendant said. "I'll call him for you." She picked up a pager and dialed a number. A few seconds later, Paul responded. "There are three young ladies here to see you, Paul."

"Be right there, as soon as I finish with my patient."

"You can wait in the visitor's lounge." The attendant directed them around the corner to a sitting room filled with chairs and tables arranged in groups, various vending machines, coffee pots, and two doors labeled "Men" and "Ladies." The wear and tear on the furniture implied that it had been years since the last update. It smelled of stale coffee and disinfectant.

They sat in the chairs closest to the lounge entrance and waited fifteen minutes until a chubby-looking man in his mid-twenties popped his head through the doorway. "Are you the ladies looking for Paul?"

"Yes," Maddie said. They stood to meet him. "Are you James Bond?"

"You must be Maddie." Paul extended his hand for a handshake.

"These are my friends, Val and Wynona."

"I'm pleased to meet you, ladies. I wasn't expecting to receive my next assignment so soon. How can I help you?"

"I need to see Frankie. Can you get me into CCU?" Maddie asked.

"Um. That would be against hospital rules," he said. He stuck his hand out and rubbed his fingers together as if to say "For a fee."

Maddie opened her purse, found a five-dollar bill and placed it on his palm. He wadded the bill, shoved it into his lab coat pocket and turned his back toward them. After taking two steps forward, he glanced over his shoulder with the most casual of airs and feigned a British accent. He said, "*Two* nurses and *one* doctor are attending *forty-four* patients today. They're looking dapper in their *white lab coats and blue name tags*. I take my break in the employee lounge at 3:30. Perhaps you will to join me for a soda? Good day, ladies."

"Remember two, one, four, four, Val. That must be the buzz-in code."

Wynona looked at her wrist watch. "It's 3:20. Since you worked here, you should know where the employee lounge is."

"Follow me." Maddie motioned them down the hall to the right. "We'll have to wait until the nurse's station is unmanned."

The girls trailed Paul down the hallway, lagging ten paces back. He went into the lounge; Maddie, Wynona, and Val kept going past the nurse's station. A nurse hung up the phone, picked up a tray of medications and went into a patient's room. Maddie watched through the corner of her eye. She waited for a second nurse, reading a patient chart attached to a clipboard, to move away from the station. It seemed as if she would never move. When she did, the first nurse came back out of the patient room with an empty tray.

"No," Maddie whispered. "Please go the other way."

The nurse headed straight toward them but walked on past the station to another patient room. Maddie sprinted toward the lounge door and ducked inside, leaving Val and Wynona to stand guard.

"Where are you, Paul?" she whispered.

Paul peeked out from behind a door marked "Private," and motioned for her to enter. She slipped inside.

"This is the doctor's lounge. Doctor Johnson leaves her lab coat in here when she's in surgery. She should be gone for another hour or two. Take her coat and badge and put your hair up in this surgical cap. Turn your head away from the attendant when you go through the unit doors. Families may visit for fifteen minutes every two hours. The next visit is at 4:00 p.m. If you hurry, you can be in and out before then. Don't get caught."

Paul cracked the door just wide enough to peer into the employee lounge, then opened it wider and left. Maddie put on the coat and hat, then slipped out behind him. She tucked her chin and cleared her throat to get Val and Wynona's attention, but they were watching for incoming personnel. "*Umh, Umh, Umh.*" She coughed louder. Val recognized Maddie's shoes and poked Wynona in the arm to alert her.

"You are crazy, Maddie! If you get caught in that get-up, they will haul you out of here in the paddy wagon."

"Shh, pretend we're not together, and follow me. I need you to make sure the family doesn't get in there until I come back out." Maddie looked down at the clipboard in her hand as if studying it.

"Just how are we supposed to do that?" Wynona asked in a whisper. "I am not doing this!"

"Come on, Wynona," Val said. "You owe Maddie this much for putting up with you. She'd do it for you." She fell in line a few steps behind Maddie.

Wynona walked fast to catch up to Val. "You better not get caught, Maddie Randall. If you do, I'm out of here."

At the CCU doors, Maddie lifted her hand to punch in the code. "What was that number? Did you remember it?"

"Two nurses, one doctor, and forty-four patients," Val said.

"What time is it, Wynona?"

"It's three-forty-five. You have fifteen minutes, so be out in ten."

Maddie took a deep breath and shook her arms to lessen the tension, then pushed the code number on the keypad. A loud buzzer sounded and the double doors sprung wide. Beds, separated by green-striped curtains hung on overhead tracks, were lined up in rows on both sides of the room. She tiptoed through, peering behind each curtain until she found a patient wrapped in a body cast. Gauze bandages covered his face except for two eye openings, a tiny hole where the nose should be, and a slit at the mouth. *This has to be Frankie.*

She tiptoed to the side of the bed and whispered, "Frankie, can you hear me?" Tears clouded her vision.

He didn't respond, so she touched his fingers protruding from the end of the cast on his left arm. "Frankie, it's Maddie. I don't know if you can hear me, but I need you to understand that I don't blame you for what you did. This is my fault too. If I hadn't allowed you to touch me, this would never have happened. Please, get better. I will pray for you every day."

Maddie held to his fingers and prayed. "Abba, Frankie said he doesn't believe you are God's son, but I do. Please, Abba, make Frankie well and touch his heart so he will want to know you. Amen."

As Maddie turned to go, Frankie's fingers twitched. "Frankie, are you awake?" She peered into the eye openings and saw him blink. "Blink twice if you can hear me, Frankie."

He blinked twice. He pressed together the thumb and index finger of his right hand as if he were holding a pencil and pretended to write. "Do you want a pencil?"

He blinked twice. Maddie grabbed the half-size pen hanging from Frankie's chart on the wall and placed it in his fingers. She held the chart as still as she could beneath the pen. A tear formed in the corner of Frankie's eye.

A loud buzz sounded and the double doors opened. *Oh, no! I have to get out of here.* No one noticed her as she grabbed the chart and shuffled past the group of weary-eyed visitors who savored the few minutes of time allotted to them with their dearest loved ones.

"What took you so long?" Val whispered without moving her lips as they walked. Maddie didn't answer. They walked faster and faster until they turned the corner at the end of the hall. Then she stripped off the surgical cap and lab coat. They didn't stop until they reached the elevator.

"Did you see him, Maddie? Could he talk to you?" Wynona wouldn't hush.

"I saw him, but he couldn't talk. He is in a body cast and his head is covered with bandages except for his eyes and nostrils." The elevator stopped on the ground floor and the doors opened. Maddie took the chart and dropped the board on the floor in the corner. "Let's go."

CHAPTER 19

Maddie's heart ached. She wished she hadn't seen Frankie in that condition. The image of him wrapped like a mummy haunted her. His fingers moved, and his eyes, but what about the rest of his body? And what about his legs? Would he ever walk again? She wished she'd had more time.

She pulled the page she had taken from the chart board from her handbag and flattened it in the light from the lamp on her dressing table. She took out the tiny magnifying glass she kept on her key ring and tried to decipher Frankie's scribbling. *So sorry,* then a wavy line that trailed off down the page.

She turned the chart over and read his name. Franklin Z. Mason III.

The next morning Maddie got up early and drove to St. John's before going to school. She put the chart in a plain white envelope, labeled it "Critical Care Unit-Mason," and placed it inside a magazine. She took the elevator to the second floor CCU lounge. A slouched woman with tired eyes shuffled out of the restroom and sat at the table near the coffee pot. She paid no attention to Maddie. Maddie sidled to the desk in the corner and placed the envelope next to the phone.

"May I help you?" asked a voice behind her.

"I'm looking for the surgical lounge. Am I in the right place?"

"No, ma'am. Surgery is on the third floor."

"Thank you," she said, and hurried out. At the end of the hall she turned the corner, raced to the stairs, and descended them two at a time. She slowed her pace as she crossed the lobby and passed through the exterior doors leading to the parking lot.

***

"I have news," Wynona said when Maddie arrived at school just before the eight o'clock bell rang. "Word is the hospital is looking for the person who stole Frankie's chart. They said they won't press charges if the person who took it will just return it."

"That's why I'm late. I took it back this morning and left it at the desk in the lounge."

Wynona's mouth gaped. "Maddie, you are brave, or out of your mind."

"I feel responsible for what happened to Frankie, and I couldn't risk them overdosing him because they didn't have his chart."

Wynona wrinkled her forehead. "Why do you feel responsible?"

Maddie nibbled at her lower lip. "We, uh, fought the night Frankie wrecked. He may have been angry."

"Well, if he drove too fast because he was angry, that doesn't make it your fault he wrecked. He's the one who made the choice, Maddie. No one can blame you, and you shouldn't blame yourself either."

"I guess you're right," Maddie said, glad Wynona hadn't probed for more details.

After school Val and Maddie met in the school library. "What are you looking for?" Val asked when Maddie headed for the newspaper archives.

"Franklin Z. Mason, Senior or Junior. There's no listing in the phone directory for either, and I'm curious. Wynona mentioned a senator named Mason. Let's start there."

Twenty minutes into their research, Val said, "Hey Mads, come here and look at this."

Looking over Val's shoulder at the newspaper article, Maddie gasped. "Oh my Lord, have mercy! He looks like an older version of Frankie!"

Val scanned the article for details. "This guy, Dr. Zachariah Mason, runs the East Side Medical Clinic. He is accused of selling

Schedule II controlled drugs to college students. It doesn't say if they arrested him."

"Isn't that the clinic next to our school? Does it say where he lives, or if he has family?"

Maddie remembered the day she had stepped off the curb without looking, and Frankie had almost hit her. *He seemed exhilarated after running into the ditch and barely missing a power pole. Had he been high then?*

"There's not much else here. We can search for articles on the clinic, but we'll have to do it later. The librarian has turned out the lights up front. I guess that's our cue she's closing. We can go to the public library Saturday morning."

***

Saturday morning Cal was up before Maddie, banging his hammer against the wall outside her bedroom window. She covered her head with her pillow, but the hammering vibrated the window panes. *No more sleep today.*

She rolled out of bed and ambled into the kitchen where Belva was cleaning the oven. "What is Cal doing out there? Tearing down the back wall?" She rubbed her eyes and slumped into the chair nearest her.

"Good morning, Maddie. There's bacon and biscuits for you in the bowl on the back of the range, and there's fresh coffee in the pot. I'm sorry he woke you so early. After visiting the home show with Jim last week he got excited about a billiard room. Do you remember last summer when Mr. Hadley gave him the used materials from his old barn if Cal would haul it away? He hauled it away and piled it up in our back yard. I'm happy he's doing something with it."

Maddie poured herself a cup of coffee and carried the bowl of breakfast to the table. "A billiard room? We don't have a pool table. Does Cal even play?"

"I guess he plans to learn." Belva hummed as she wiped the greasy cleaning foam from the oven door.

Maddie ate breakfast, then wandered out back to take a look at Cal's handiwork. "Hand me that box of nails from off the window sill, Maddie. I'm making us a place to play pool. What do you think?"

"It sounds fine," she said, supposing it to be another of Cal's unfinished projects. She placed the box of nails on the top platform of the step ladder. "I need to ask you something, Daddy. When you talked to Frankie the night he brought me home from the park, what did you say to him?"

Cal's countenance fell, and he stopped hammering. "After what he did to you, I thought you'd be through with him."

"I am. I want to know what you said to him."

"He's not who you think he is. Take my word for it and stay away from him."

Cal turned his back to Maddie and went back to hammering even louder. She went back inside and asked Belva. "Did Cal tell you how he knows Frankie?"

"No, he didn't."

Back in her bedroom, Maddie closed the window curtains and pulled on her favorite jeans. She reached for her favorite "Midnight Cowboy" tee shirt, then shoved it back into the drawer and wore her plain blue tank top instead. She brushed her hair and pushed it away from her face with a wide elastic white headband, then left for the library.

Val met her on the library steps. "Let's not go in there today, Maddie. I have something to tell you."

"What is it, Val? What's wrong?"

Val frowned and led her to the wooden bench beside the red, white, and blue public mail box. "Let's sit over here at the bus stop." She sat for a minute or two then fastened her eyes to Maddie's and tried to speak, but the words hung in her throat. A deep breath and a sigh later, she tried again. "It's about Frankie."

"What about Frankie?" Maddie sensed this was about more than Frankie's family tree.

"There's an article in the newspaper this morning, Mads. Frankie died last night."

"What? No! No! No! That can't be true!" Maddie drew her knees up to her chin and held her forehead against them with her fingers laced behind her head. She sobbed and mourned while Val held her, rocking back and forth.

CHAPTER 20

Maddie drove to Mountainside Park alone and found a quiet spot on a bench near the lake. She sat for hours, pondering. The sun's reflection off the ducks' teal feathers cast a greenish blue hue on the water that resembled an artist's rendition of nature in perfect harmony. Dozens of multicolored ducks played follow-the-leader from the shore to the center of the lake and then back again. "Life for them is orchestrated and simplistic with no thoughts beyond the moment," she thought.

"Abba, where are you? I need you."

"I've never left you, Maddie." A gentle warmth soothed her hurting heart.

"I prayed for You to make Frankie well and help him want to give his heart to You. Now he's gone, and it's too late. Why, Abba? I don't understand."

"Be still, my child. Peace will find you."

"I don't have peace except in You, Lord. I wish my life was as simple as the life of those ducks out there on the lake. They are satisfied to follow along behind their leader. Why can't it be that way for people too?"

"My child, it can be. Come, follow me."

Maddie lifted her eyes toward heaven and said, "I'm trying, Lord. Please help me."

The sun's rays found Maddie's face and dried her tears. "Thank You, Abba." A compelling urge to talk to Belva drew her homeward.

***

"You've been crying, Maddie, and it's been hours since you left for the library. What is the matter?" Belva coaxed her daughter to sit and talk.

"Frankie is dead, Momma." Maddie slumped into Belva's arms and moaned sorrowful sobs again. "It's in the morning newspaper. I needed time alone, so I went to the park and stayed longer than I meant to."

"Oh, Maddie, I'm so sorry." She patted her daughter on the back.

"I don't understand, Momma. When I went to the hospital to see him, his whole body was broken, but he was awake. I never thought he was dying. I can't believe he's gone. Frankie didn't believe in Jesus, Momma. I wanted to help him believe, but I couldn't, and now it's too late."

"You're a good person with a good heart, Maddie, but you can't make someone believe. It's a choice they have to make."

Maddie lifted her head off Belva's shoulder and backed away. She reached for a tissue from the box on the coffee table and dabbed her nose. "Frankie had a good heart too. He would never have behaved the way he did if it wasn't for the drugs."

"He was using drugs?" Belva asked, her curiosity piqued.

"He was always courteous and polite until that night at the movies. His personality changed after he'd been to the restrooms. That's when he . . ."

Unwilling to relive the horrible night, Maddie said, "Frankie never talked about his family. When I couldn't find their names in the phone directory, Val and I searched the newspaper archives trying to find information about them. We found an article about Dr. Zachariah Mason who had been accused of selling illegal drugs to college students a few months ago. He looked like an older Frankie. We were going back to the library today to look for more. But after reading the article in today's paper, we knew then that Zachariah was Frankie's grandfather. Is that what Cal wouldn't tell me?"

"I suppose it's possible."

"If they've done something illegal that got Frankie killed, they shouldn't be allowed to get away with it. I wonder how many more people have died, or had their lives ruined, because of their drugs. I'm going back to the library to see what else I can find out about the Masons."

"Maddie, please don't dig around in something that will get you hurt. Drug dealers are unscrupulous and dangerous."

"I know," Maddie said. "But library research isn't dangerous."

***

By the following weekend, the reality of it all fell heavy around Maddie. A dark, stormy mass of depression separated her so far from the light of hope. She wanted to sink into the depths of her mattress and hide from the sunshine that floated through her bedroom window. **Even the** smell of bacon and fresh coffee didn't tempt her today. Belva called her to breakfast, but she pulled the covers over her head to muffle the sounds of Cal shuffling through the house, slamming cabinet doors and drawers. *Please don't hammer on the walls again today.*

When Maddie didn't answer, Belva came into the room. "Maddie, honey, you need to get up and eat something before breakfast gets cold."

"I don't want to, Momma. I want to go back to sleep so I don't have to think. My head hurts, and I'm so tired."

"Lying in bed won't make it go away, Maddie." Belva sat on the edge of the bed and tugged at the covers her daughter had cocooned around herself. "Come on out of there. I'm going back to the kitchen now, but if you don't get up and follow me, I'm coming back with a big glass of ice water."

There was no sleeping in if Momma said it's time to get up, and Maddie had experienced the ice-water motivator the last time she tried to sleep in. Belva would hold the glass above her head and let it drip, drip, drip, until the covers were so wet she had no choice but to get up. She despised the trick, but deep down, she knew Belva was right to keep her moving. So she forced herself to unwind from the covers and slide her feet to the floor.

The mirror exposed her sorrow by reflecting the deep, dark half-moons encircling her eyes like puffy storm clouds and the fiery lightning bolts streaking through the whites of her eyes. *Maybe a hot bath will help?*

Maddie wished Cal had finished plumbing the bathroom. The tiny closet of a room had a commode and an old tub with an iron pipe protruding from the wall above it. Attached to the end of the pipe was a piece of water hose and a spray nozzle. He never installed a hot water heater. Before bathing she had to boil water in a kettle on the range, pour it into the tub, then mix cold water into it to cool it to a comfortable temperature. Or she could take an icy shower. Today she needed a long, indulgent bubble bath. So she padded her way to the kitchen to put the kettle on.

Maddie took two aspirins and sipped a cup of hot coffee. By the time the water boiled in the pot, her, head had stopped pounding and she was ready to slide into the tub. Cal yelled from somewhere outside, "Someone bring me a shirt." That meant he was leaving. He always covered his tank-type undershirt with a button-up before going out. She took a potholder from the drawer and carried her hot water to the bathroom before he yelled a second time.

"Please, Momma," she thought, "take him a shirt and send him away."

The bathroom had no window, so she turned out the light and let the total darkness and the warm, bubbly water ease away the stress. Tranquil visions of treasured moments drifted through her thoughts: the aroma of Frankie's aftershave on the day he'd helped her get Mr. Smith off the hospital floor, and the look on his face the night Wynona barfed on his sandals. Sweet endearments floated above her in the fog of steam encircling the tub. So much had changed in such a short time. From sweetest memories to lurid nightmares, the events unfolded until the whole of it engulfed her spirit in a dense, gloomy fog.

An hour later Maddie emerged from the tub waterlogged. Her toes and fingers looked and felt like shriveled persimmons when she flipped the light switch on. She dried herself on the fluffy bunny-soft bath towel Belva had hung beside the tub, then wrapped it around her hair, turban-style.

Cal knocked on the bathroom door. "Are you staying in there all day? Hurry up!"

"I'm coming out now." She slipped into her lavender, chenille robe and opened the door to see him standing there with his hands propped, one on each side of the doorway, huffing. She didn't have the strength to squabble with him today so she slipped by him without a word. *Why didn't he stay away longer?*

***

Nature lifted her eyes toward heaven as dawn coaxed the day awake. Granny Nettie's old rocking chair creak, creak, creaked, a gentle rhythm as Maddie swayed back and forth. The front porch on Sunday at dawn, when the world lay silent and still, found her in reverent worship, enjoying the Holy Spirit descending around her. Though He spoke not an audible word, the echo of His silence breathed restoration and newness of life into her anesthetized soul. She was still rocking when Belva turned on the kitchen light and made the coffee.

CHAPTER 21

"Please don't do that." Val pleaded with Maddie to consider the consequences of her plan. "It's too dangerous. I've read horrible stories about addicts and drug pushers. You're getting into something deep and dangerous."

"I intend to find out if Dr. Mason is selling illegal drugs. If he is, he needs to be stopped before more people die." Maddie clutched the steering wheel with an obstinate grip. "If you won't help me, I'll find someone who will."

Val rocked forward in her seat and planted her palms on the dashboard with a smack. "Why don't you talk to the police! Isn't that their job?"

"And what would I say?" Maddie glowered at her. "My dead boyfriend was taking drugs and they should check it out? No, I've scheduled an appointment at East Side Clinic with Dr. Mason for four o'clock Thursday afternoon. If he is selling drugs without prescriptions, I will get him to sell them to me. And when he does, then I'll go to the police. Are you going with me, or not?"

Val shook her head in an absolute no. "I won't go, Maddie, and neither should you."

"Fine, then I'll ask Wynona." Maddie kept her eyes straight ahead and never spoke another word until they arrived at school. "I'll see you at lunch," she said, and trotted into the building.

***

At lunch, Maddie petitioned Wynona in the cafeteria when they sat to eat. "I need you to go with me to the East Side Clinic on Thursday afternoon to get cocaine and amphetamines. Will you go?" Wynona opened her milk carton and ripped the wrapper off the plastic cutlery.

"What? You're kidding me, right?"

"No," Maddie said. "I am dead serious. I believe Frankie was taking drugs, and I believe he got them from his grandpa at the clinic. I'm going over there to find out."

Wynona giggled. "How do you plan to do that---sit on him and twist his arm until he confesses?"

"No, I plan to get him to sell drugs to me. Then I'll report him to the authorities."

"Are you crazy stupid? Or just crazy out of your mind? You can't just walk in there and demand drugs."

Maddie made a disgusted face at the pile of mushy meat on her plate. "How can they call this meatloaf?" She pushed it aside and plunged her fork into the mashed potatoes. "I'll find a way to do it. I'm not sure how yet, but I will."

"Why are you so all-fired independent, Maddie? You know I won't let you go over there alone, and I know you won't quit until you find out. So I'll go with you, but if you make trouble for yourself, I won't be a part of it. I have enough problems."

Maddie guzzled her chocolate milk to the bottom of the carton and dumped her meatloaf into the garbage can. "You're the best, Wynona."

"Yeah, the best and biggest sucker in the county." She dropped her apple into her purse, dumped the trash, and put her tray atop the fifteen others on the rolling cart beside the garbage can. "Gotta love your spunk though."

Over the next three days, Maddie planned how to approach Dr. Mason. It had to look real, or he might become suspicious. She'd transform herself into a hippie with ragged jeans, leather sandals, sunglasses, a tie-dyed tee shirt, and flowers in her hair. She could tell him Frankie used to bring her drugs.

***

"Please fill these out and bring them back when you're finished." The receptionist handed her a clipboard loaded with forms while eyeing her from top to toe and shaking her head in disapproval. Maddie heard her whisper to the other woman in the office, "Another pot-head hippie."

She started to write her name at the top of the forms, then remembered not to use her real name. *Joanna Smith*, she printed with precise lettering. She falsified her address and Social Security number, birthdate, and reason for visit, then handed them back to the receptionist.

"Thank you, Miss—Smith," she said, and peered over the top of her round, wire-rimmed glasses. "Have a seat in the lobby, and the doctor will be with you soon."

Fifteen minutes passed, then thirty. The lobby was full with waiting patients. Two had been there when she arrived, and five or six more came in after her. Maddie played with the frayed edges around the holes in her jeans and chewed the ear piece on her psychedelic patterned sunglasses. *I wish Wynona had come inside with me.* She had almost lost her nerve when a swinging door opened and a nurse called, "Jones, Baker, Smith." The two people who had been there when Maddie arrived rose and followed the nurse through the door. "Smith—anyone here named Joanna Smith?"

Maddie looked around the room then remembered. "I am Joanna Smith," she said, and followed her down the hallway. The nurse led her to a tiny room and directed her to sit on the edge of an examination table while she took her temperature and blood pressure. "Your chart says you have an ear ache, is that correct?"

She touched her left ear and said, "Yeah, I need something for pain."

The nurse scribbled something at the top of the chart and dropped it into a plastic bin attached to the door. "Doctor Hudson will be in soon."

"No, wait! Not Dr. Hudson. I want Dr. Mason."

"Dr. Hudson can treat an ear infection just fine, Miss Smith."

"But it's important that I see Dr. Mason." Maddie slid herself off the edge of the table. "I'll come back whenever he's in. When will he be here?"

"Why is it so important that you see Dr. Mason? He's very busy and he can't treat every patient."

"It's just that Dr. Mason's grandson, Frankie, was a friend of mine and he used to *help* me."

"Uh-huh," the nurse muttered. "I'll ask if he's got time to talk to you since you're a friend of Frankie's."

"Groovy," Maddie said, popping her gum. "Peace, my friend."

Twenty minutes later, someone knocked on the door. Before Maddie could respond, a white-haired man with a Colonel Sanders moustache stuck his head into the room. "I'm Dr. Mason. So you were Frankie's friend?" he asked, with a doubtful smirk.

"Yeah, Frankie was the best. He never disappointed me when I needed, eh, help." Maddie spit out her gum and rolled it between her fingers then tossed it toward the trash can, but missed. She opened a fresh stick of Juicy Fruit, picked up the dropped gum and wadded it into the wrapper.

Dr. Mason rubbed his chin and studied her face. "How did Frankie help you, Miss Smith?"

"How? You know how. He said you made sure he had plenty of help to give. If you know what I mean." She wrung her hands from genuine anxiety and hoped he thought it was because she needed a fix.

"Miss Smith, if you're looking for drugs then I'm afraid you may have misunderstood

Frankie. You need to leave now before I call the police. If *you* know what *I* mean." He opened the door and gestured for her to leave.

"Frankie said you were a man with a heart, and you helped people get what they need. Forget I asked. I'll find someone else to help me." She bounded off the exam table, looked Dr. Mason straight in the eye, and curled her lip in a smirk. "I guess I'm not your kind."

As soon as she reached the lobby, she ran out the door and around the corner to the supermarket parking lot where Wynona waited. "What happened in there? What took you so long?" Wynona asked.

"Let's just get out of here." Maddie pulled out of the parking lot and into the traffic on Main Street. She didn't notice the black pickup truck that pulled out from East Side Clinic and slipped into the traffic two cars behind her.

"What happened in there, Maddie?" Wynona asked again.

"Nothing happened. That's the problem. Dr. Mason threatened to call the police, but I don't buy it. I'll bet he's checking me out this minute."

"Please tell me you didn't give him your real name and address."

"I didn't. I'm not an idiot. There's got to be another way to catch him."

"No, Maddie! If he is selling illegal drugs, then he's dangerous and you could get hurt. If he's not, he'll have you arrested for harassing him." She clasped her hands together, pressed them between her knees, and rocked back and forth.

"Don't worry, Wynona. I'll be fine."

"I do worry, Maddie. Please, stop this nonsense. I couldn't bear it if something bad happened to you."

Maddie swayed the car toward the right side of the road to allow a speeding pickup truck to pass her on the narrow dirt road to Wynona's house. "Someone's in a hurry," she said when the dust boiled up in front of her.

"What a jerk," Wynona said. She fanned her face to keep the dust from entering her nostrils.

Maddie pulled into the driveway at the Wade residence and left the engine running while Wynona got out. "Thanks for going with me," she said. "See you at school tomorrow."

"Sure, Maddie, no problem. You're always praying, so why don't you pray for wisdom tonight? Maybe you'll wake up wiser in the morning and give up on this crazy quest of yours."

"I will pray about it, Wynona, and I'm glad you understand that prayer works."

Maddie left Wynona's at five-thirty p.m. and stopped at the market for a soda before heading for home. *I look ridiculous in this hippie garb. Daniel will laugh me out of the store when he sees me, but I don't care. I'm so thirsty I could drink a bucketful of lake water.* She pulled her Carmen Ghia into a parking space beside the market, reached for her handbag, and opened the car door to get out when a rough, smelly hand capped itself over her mouth. Her world went black.

Chapter 22

Belva paced the floor, waiting for Cal to call her back. Fifteen minutes passed and still no phone call. Something terrible had happened to Maddie, and she couldn't stop pacing the floor waiting for Cal to call. The phone rang the instant she reached for it to call for the police. "Thank you, God."

"Hello, Cal?"

"What's so important it couldn't wait until I get home? I'm not supposed to take calls during work hours."

"I know, Cal, but something has happened to Maddie. Daniel called and told me her car is parked beside his store with her keys still in the ignition and the door wide open. Her handbag was on the ground beside it. I need you here with me, Cal. Will you please come home?"

"Have you called those two friends of hers? Maybe she's with them."

Belva's voice quivered. "I talked to Wynona. She said Maddie dropped her off at home at five-thirty. It was six-thirty when Daniel called. She would never leave her handbag on the ground or her keys in the ignition, Cal."

"That girl can get herself into more trouble than a raccoon in a bakery. Call the sheriff," Cal said and hung up the phone.

Belva dialed the number for emergencies pasted to the underside of the handset.

"Sheriff's office." A professional-sounding woman answered.

"Hello, I'm Belva Randall. My daughter is missing. Please help me find her."

"Slow down, Mrs. Randall, and tell me how long has she been missing?"

"She never came home from school today, and our neighbor found her car parked at his store with the keys in the ignition and the door open. Her handbag was on the ground beside the car. Something has happened to her." Belva heard Cal's pendulum clock strike seven times.

"I'll radio the Sheriff and send him over there right away. What's the address of the store?"

"It's on the corner of Highway 61 West and Hill Lane. Please hurry."

***

The gag rag pressed hard against her tongue and stung the corners of her mouth. Her jaws hurt. Ropes around her wrists and ankles rubbed against her skin when she tried to wriggle free.

The cramped space was dark except for a tiny ray of light beneath a door that imparted an eerie ambience to the dank cubbyhole. The musty odor of mildew made her stomach queasy. Overhead, a broken wooden closet rod swung from a hook on the wall.

Maddie tried to stand but lost her balance and fell against the wall with a loud thump. Footsteps clomped across the wooden floor on the other side of the door then grew silent. Shadows in the light ray beneath the door raised the hairs on the back of her neck and her pulse quickened. Her body stiffened when the door swung wide, revealing a lumbering, tattooed man with hairy arms and a gun.

"Well, I'm glad you've decided to join me," he scowled. His massive fingers gripped her arms and shoved her into a large, open room. He pushed her into a ragged, damp Queen Anne-style chair. After loosening the gag, he grabbed the chair arms and dragged her forward until the two of them were nose-to-nose. She cringed and turned her head away from his putrid breath.

"Now, tell me who you are and who sent you snooping around Dr. M's place." He pressed his nose to her ear and sniffed her earlobe. "Things will be easier for both of us if you spill your guts now, before I'm forced to get nasty."

Maddie struggled against the giant hand clamped round her chin. "I didn't snoop. Frankie said he got my medicine from Dr. M., and since Frankie is gone, I hoped he would help me."

"The thing is, *Miss Smith*, I know every one of Frankie's people 'cause I'm the one who hooked him up---and you ain't one of 'em."

"You got it all wrong. I'm not a customer. Frankie gave me my medicine for being his girlfriend."

"If you was Frankie's girlfriend, how come I never seen him with you? Besides, Frankie had class. He'd not mess around with the likes of you. He could have any woman he wanted." His hand tightened against her face, intensifying the pain in her jaws.

"He didn't take me out in public. I wasn't that kind of girlfriend. We had a *personal* relationship, if you catch my drift."

The thug twisted a lock of her hair around his finger and pulled until she winced. "I got connections at the sheriff's office, and you ain't no Joanna Smith. That ugly brown car you drive is registered to Cal Randall, and this here driver's license I found in your bag says your name is Maddie Randall. Now, one more time: why did you go snooping around Dr. M's place?"

"Please let me go. I won't tell anybody, I promise."

He let go of her chin and unwound the hair from his finger. "Take a little time to think before you answer," he whispered into her ear as he twisted the rag around her neck, cutting off her air. "The next time we do this I won't be so friendly." He shoved the gag back into her mouth even tighter than before, then kicked the chair leg with the heel of his boot and left.
After hearing the door slam and a key turn in the lock, Maddie prayed. "Abba, I know You're here with me because You promised never to leave me. Please help me."

When the sound of tires crunching on gravel told her he'd left, she planted her feet on the floor and forced her weight backwards until the chair scooted. One inch at a time, she pushed the chair toward the corner where a piece of rusty sheet metal leaned against the wall.

"Please don't let him come back, Abba."

***

Sheriff Richards drove the county cruiser into the parking lot at Daniel's Market. With the red and blue lights strobing, he stopped behind the brown Carmen Ghia and got out. He bent his tall, brawny frame low and peered into the car, then turned and sauntered into the store.

"I'm looking for Daniel Hershel," he said to a group of teenaged boys playing the pinball machine in the corner. Five pairs of respectful eyes affixed themselves to the man wearing a khaki-colored uniform, a holstered gun on his belt, and a shiny badge on his chest.

"He's in the garage, sir."

"Thanks, boys."

Five apprehensive voices chimed in unison, "You're welcome."

"Hello, Sheriff Richards," Daniel extended his hand to shake. "I'm glad you're here. We're worried that something awful has happened to Maddie, and right here in my lot too."

"Tell me about Miss Randall. What kind of company does she keep?" The sheriff took a note pad and pen out of his shirt pocket.

"Maddie is a good kid. She spends most of her time at home. I've seen her with two of our other local girls, Valerie Michaels and Wynona Wade." Daniel pulled a pipe out of his shirt pocket, filled it with tobacco, and held it between his teeth without lighting it. With a match between the thumb and forefinger of his right hand, suspended half way between his waist and his chin, and his left hand cupped around the pipe bowl, he said, "I saw her a few times with that Mason fellow, before the accident."

"Which accident are you referring to, Mr. Hershel?"

"The one involving that little red sports car a few weeks back." He struck the match against the bowl of his pipe and inhaled, pulling the fire into the tobacco. "I heard the Mason guy died."

"Yeah, I remember that one." Sheriff Richards made a note on his pad. "It was the worst I'd seen. That poor fellow was nothing but a bag of loose bones when they pulled him out of that car. So you say Miss Randall had been dating Mason?"

"I think so." Smoke curled around his face and filled the air with the sweet smell of apple wood and cherries. "Her daddy, Cal Randall, wasn't too happy about it either. He said the fellow was twenty-four years old and liked high school girls. He figured that spelled trouble."

"Where do these two girls, Valerie Michaels and Wynona Wade, live?" the sheriff asked.

"I'll get you their addresses and telephone numbers. Both families run a tab here."

Sheriff Richards made his way back to Maddie's VW for a closer examination. The door was still standing open and her handbag still lay on the ground near the front tire. Sheriff Richards ambled back to his cruiser and radioed his deputy.

"Run a background check on Frankie Mason. Check for priors, then come over to Daniel's Market on Highway 61. Bring a crime scene kit with you."

"Mr. Hershel, I'm going over to visit with the two girls you said were friends of Miss Randall's. My deputy is on his way. I'd appreciate it if you'll keep an eye on this car until he gets here. Make sure no one messes with it."

"Yes, sir. I'll do whatever I can to help."

***

The sheriff knocked on Val Michaels' door and waited a minute before knocking again. No one came to the door, so he made a note of the time and returned to his vehicle. "Wynona Wade," he thought. "Where have I heard that name?"

As the Wade home came into view, he remembered Jonathan Wade, the old drunk he used to haul in every weekend to sleep it off in the jail. *I hope this girl is smarter than her old man, or her grandpa, or whoever he was.*

Mrs. Wade opened the door, surprised to see the sheriff. "Sheriff Richards, what brings you out this way? I haven't seen you since the last time John's daddy spent the night in your jail."

"Yeah, it's nice to see you again, Mrs. Wade. None of your family is under arrest this time. I need to talk to Wynona if she's home."

"She's here. She's not in any trouble, is she?"

"No, ma'am. I'm looking for information."

"Wynona! Come in here. Sheriff Richards is here, and he needs to talk to you." Mrs. Wade yelled through the house without leaving her post, then turned back to the sheriff. "Why don't you come on in, Sheriff? I'll fix you a glass of sweet tea."

Chapter 23

Belva knelt by the sofa. "Lord, I've trusted You to protect our girls since the day You gave them to us, and You always have. I trust You now and beg You to please bring Maddie back to us unharmed." She was still on her knees when Cal came through the door.

"Thank God, you're home. What are we going to do?"

"I'll go see the sheriff,"

She reached for his hand and pulled herself up from her knees. "Daniel called a few minutes ago and said Sheriff Richards had already been to the store and checked out Maddie's car."

"I'm going over to Daniel's then." He turned toward the door.

Daniel met Cal in the store parking lot. "Her car is around here, Cal. The sheriff asked me to not allow anyone to touch anything until his deputy could get here and process the scene for evidence. I'll show you what I found."

Cal followed Daniel to the side of the building. "When did you find it?" he asked.

"It was around six this afternoon. I came outside to empty the trash into the dumpster out back and found it like this. I knew right away that something had to be wrong, so I called Mrs. Randall. She called Sheriff Richards."

Cal straightened his back, sniffed, and tugged at the waist of his pants. "A man would be a lot better off with boys. At least they can half-way take care of themselves."

"Girls today are a lot different than when we were teenagers," Daniel said. He pointed to the car turning into the lot. "Here comes the deputy now."

***

"When was the last time you saw Maddie Randall?" the sheriff asked Wynona while sipping his sweet tea at Mrs. Wade's kitchen table.

"She dropped me off at home this afternoon about 5:30. Why? What's wrong?"

"Your friend is missing. Has she been in any trouble or acted different than usual?"

Wynona placed her hand over her mouth. "Oh no! I knew she was asking for trouble when she went to that clinic."

"What clinic?" Sheriff Richards looked puzzled.

"Maddie had this crazy idea that Frankie's grandpa gave him drugs. She thought Dr. Mason caused Frankie's death, so she went to his clinic and pretended to be a hippie looking for amphetamines." Wynona walked to the door and stared into the air. "She wanted to find out if he would give them to her so she could report him, but he threatened to call the police if she didn't leave."

"Back up and tell me, is this the same Frankie who died from the wreck in the sports car a few weeks ago?" She walked back to the table and sat in the chair beside her mother.

"Yes, that's Frankie Mason. Maddie had been out on a date with him the night of the wreck, and she said he acted strange after he went to the men's room. He tried to force her to, you know, do things she didn't want to do. She had been out with him before, and she said he had always been a gentleman. That's why she thought he must have taken something that night."

Sheriff Richards scratched his head. "Why would she think he got drugs from his grandfather? That seems way out there."

"She found an article in the newspaper on Dr. Zachariah Mason---that's Frankie's grandpa. Someone had accused him of selling drugs to college kids. I told her not to go in there, but she wouldn't listen."

"Thank you, Wynona. You've been a big help. At least now I have a starting place. I'll be checking out Dr. Zachariah Mason. And thank you for the tea, Mrs. Wade."

He returned to Daniel's Market and found his deputy, Cal, and Daniel still in the parking lot.

He called the deputy to the side. "Are you finished here?"

The deputy nodded. "I've inspected everything and dusted for fingerprints. Whatever happened, it must have taken Miss Randall by surprise. There's no sign of struggle other than the purse on the ground. Her driver's license is missing."

"What about the report on Frankie Mason? Did you find anything there?"

"No, sheriff. His record is clean except for a couple of speeding tickets, nothing criminal."

"Wrap it up here and tell Mr. Randall he can take his daughter's car home."

Cal stopped Sheriff Richards before he could get back in his cruiser. "Does that Wade girl know anything about this?" he asked.

The sheriff got into the car and close the door. "Mr. Randall, there's nothing I can tell you right now. When I have something solid, you'll be the first to know."

When the taillights from the cruiser faded out of sight, Cal headed in the opposite direction to see Wynona Wade.

***

The rusty sheet metal chewed away at the ropes on Maddie's wrists as she scraped them across the razor-sharp, jagged edges. *One slip and it could all* be over. "Slow and steady," she told herself. "I can do this." She sawed and sawed, cutting one strand of rope at a time until the knot broke free, then she pulled the gag from her mouth and untied the binding from around her ankles. The ropes had rubbed her wrists and ankles raw, and tiny droplets of blood trickled onto her hands and feet.

"I have to get out of here," she thought. "But where is here? How far away from home am I?"

The space had unfinished wooden floors with knot holes and nail heads protruding through the boards. Three walls of slatted boards, splattered with red paint and filthy graffiti were covered with old newspapers that had been eaten away by rats or other rodents. Another wall had several large sheets of plywood tacked to it with rusty nails. *I wonder if that plywood is covering the windows. There must be something around here that I can use to pry those loose.*

She remembered the broken rod hanging in the closet and ran to get it. With some difficulty, she wrangled it free from its hook and carried it to the boarded-up wall. She forced the rod underneath the edge of the smallest board where the nails had loosened, and pried at it until she felt it give. One nail popped loose, then another and another, until the bottom and both sides sprung free. The window was there. She dragged the ratty, Queen Ann chair over to the wall and used it as a stepping stool, then pried at the nails on the top edge until the board fell to the floor.

A four-foot square, single-paned window with a crack running from the top to the bottom broke into large pieces when she pressed the corner of the plywood into it. With the broken closet-rod she knocked away the jagged edges, then stood on the back of the old chair and climbed out. When her feet touched the ground, she ran into the woods and didn't stop until darkness crept in. Hoot owls, tiny varmints scurrying through the night, and dogs barking in the distance intensified her sense of being alone and afraid.

Maddie fell to her knees, turned her face toward heaven and begged. "Abba, Abba, please help me." Then she gathered her courage and walked toward a light shining through the trees in front of her. The light brightened and the sound of traffic roared in the distance. She forged ahead to a clearing and found herself in a field with a barn at the far end of it. It was the place where Frankie had taken her. *But where is the light that led me here?*

Chapter 24

Cal came sliding into Wynona's driveway and bounded out of the car onto the front porch. He pounded on the front door until Wynona answered it. In response to his grilling, Wynona told him about the East Side Clinic and Maddie's plan to expose Dr. Mason's drug operations.

"Did you notice anything unusual at the clinic, or maybe someone following you after you left?" Cal asked.

"No." She balled her hands into fists and tapped them together. She rocked backward and forward in a rhythmic sway. "We were in a hurry to get out of there. The only thing that might have been out of the ordinary was when we turned off the main highway. A pickup truck went around going fast. If Maddie hadn't noticed him when she did he would have forced us off the road."

Cal leaned closer and closer to Wynona and raised his hands to reach for her, then lowered them back to his side. "What color was the truck? Did you notice what make it was, or who was driving it?" He breathed hard and fast and his face grew redder and redder.

Wynona didn't like his distraught expression. *Was he going to grab her and shake her?* She took one step backward. "It was black with a white camper top over the bed, and I'm confident it was a Chevy. It had that little bowtie emblem on the back of it." She wrinkled her forehead and bit her lower lip, wishing he would stop leaning toward her.

"Have you seen it around here before, Wynona?" He relaxed his facial muscles and moved out of her personal space.

"No. I don't think so." She let out the breath she'd been holding.

"Can you remember anything else?"

"The driver was big. He made me think of one of those men in the movies who throw people through windows."

A wave of anger crept across his face like a shadow when he said, "I will find that doctor." Without so much as a goodbye, he went back out the door and ran toward his car.

***

Cal opened the glove compartment and removed his loaded .38 caliber Smith and Wesson revolver. He placed it on the seat beside him and sped off on the graveled road toward the main highway, leaving a blinding cloud of dust behind him.

Fifteen minutes later, he entered the Maystown city limits and turned right off Main Street at the city's one traffic light. The clinic stood one block to the east. He drove around the block looking for vehicles parked in the lot and almost didn't see it. A glint of light from his head lamps bounced off the shiny bumper of a black pickup truck with a white camper top parked in the alley between the building and the dumpster.

He turned off his lights, drove back around the block, and parked on the corner. Darkness loomed inside the building, and every step he took into the shadowed alley echoed through the stillness. There was not another sound anywhere except the howl of a dog from somewhere down the street. He sidled between the vehicle and the alley wall and hunkered next to the passenger side door. He pushed down on the handle. The door squeaked when it opened, and he held his breath. The glove compartment was unlocked, so he rifled through the mess of papers and trash until he found the registration. From the street light at the end of the alley, he could make out the name and address: Gilbert Tolstory, 412 Hickory Hollow Road. On the floorboard, a card lay face-side down near the gearshift. He flipped it over. Maddie's driver's license!

***

"Don't go off half-cocked and make matters worse by getting into trouble yourself," Belinda said to Jim while he ranted.

"Sheriff Richards better hope he finds the swine before I do!" Jim stomped through the backdoor in a fizz and let it bang closed.

His rifle hung in plain sight on a gun-rack in the back window of his truck cab. He kept a full box of ammo beneath the seat. Gravel slung out behind the back tires of his camo-painted pickup. Belinda cringed when one of them popped against the window. She prayed a silent prayer for his protection, but she didn't ask God to stop him.

***

Jim barreled across Burke Road, squealing his tires in the curves. "If he's hurt Maddie, I will personally send him flying into eternity." He let go of a string of curse words that Belinda would have reprimanded him for if she had been there.

As his truck rounded the bend, he saw Cal headed toward him, flashing his headlights and waving his arms. "I think I know who kidnapped Maddie," Cal said. "I found his truck at East Side Clinic with Maddie's driver's license in the floorboard. The truck is registered to Gilbert Tolstory on Hic . . ."

"I might just know where she is. There's an old abandoned homestead on the Tolstory place that's surrounded by woods and brush." Jim revved his engine and shoved the gear stick into reverse.

"I'll follow you, Jim. God help the man when I find him."

Jim turned his truck around and took a left off Burke onto a narrow dirt road hidden by massive clumps of kudzu, wild grapevines and honeysuckle. He knew every cave, hunting shack, cabin, barn, and abandoned building, and every pig trail, back road, and passage way that led to them.

A quarter mile from the shack, Jim and Cal turned off their headlights and engines. Cal checked his revolver and Jim took his rifle as they slipped through the trees toward their mark. Whether to Jim and Cal---or to their prey---the owls hooted a solemn word of warning.

The faint glow of candle light glimmered through an opening in the side of the abandoned farm house. They edged their way around the perimeter of the clearing. Muffled voices from within grew clearer as they inched closer. "You stupid, hair-brained idiot! You couldn't even take care of one puny little hippie girl? Why didn't you get rid of her like I told you?"

Cal and Jim eased closer and split up. A second voice whined, "I didn't want to hurt her if I didn't have to, boss. I figured she might fess-up if I threatened her and let her ponder over it for a time. How was I supposed to know she was smart enough to get loose from the ropes? Most blondes ain't got the sense God gave a turkey."

"Well, it appears God gave this one more sense than He gave you. Now get out there and find her!"

The backdoor was padlocked. Cal circled around to where he could see Jim positioned flat against the wall by the door. He stationed himself near the corner. The door opened and a tall, burly man stepped out onto the porch. Jim cocked his rifle and poked it into the man's ribs.

"Don't move, or I'll blow your lungs out through your nose," he whispered into the man's ear. "Put your hands behind your head and keep quiet if you want to live to see daylight." Jim poked his ribs harder and forced him off the porch.

The husky fellow laughed at his one-hundred and twenty-pound captor and rammed his elbow backward toward Jim's ribcage. The last thing Gilbert Tolstory saw before his world went dark was the gray steel of Jim's rifle barrel crashing into his forehead.

Cal eased onto the front porch and peered through the open door. Zachariah Mason stood glaring at the ragged chair by the broken window and the sliced ropes lying in the floor beside the rusty sheet metal. "I should have done this myself. That numbskull couldn't stick his finger up his nose without missing his nostril."

"I'm not so sure you could either," Cal said, mocking him. Cal raised his arm to aim just as Zachariah spun around and knocked the pistol out of his hand. The gun slid to the opposite side of the room. Cal pounced on him. They scuffled across the floor, each struggling against the other to gain control. The gun now lay inches away from Cal's hand. He reached to grab it. Dr. Mason pounded into Cal's face with his fist, and blood splattered red patterns across the doctor's gray pin-striped designer suit. Cal fell backward from the force of the .38 caliber bullet that rammed through his left shoulder.

Doctor Mason ran for the door but stopped cold when the bone in his nose cracked against the heel of Jim's hand. Zachariah's head jerked backwards. He fell sprawling across the floor. The back of his head slammed against a loose nail that protruded from a floor board. He never got back up.

"Lord, have mercy!" Jim squalled, and ran to see if Cal was still breathing. "Thank God!" Cal moaned and grabbed his shoulder. "Did they get away?"

"Not a chance, Cal Randall." Jim shoved his hands into his pockets, expanded his chest and boasted. "Them two suckers will have headaches for a lo-o-ong time."

Jim dragged Dr. Mason and his thug to the edge of the clearing and tied them to an oak tree with the rope he kept in his toolbox for tying deer. "They should rest there just fine until the sheriff can get over here. My guess is they will both be out for a while. Let's get you to the hospital," he said to Cal.

"No." Cal tried to stand up. "I have to find Maddie first. She's out there somewhere and she may be hurt. My shoulder can wait."

Jim helped Cal to his feet and led him back to the pickup. He keyed the mike on his CB radio. "This is Camo Jim---any of you roadrunners out there listening? I need a smoky and a meat wagon."

Cal laughed. "What did you just ask for?"

Jim grinned. "I guess you're not road savvy, pappy-n-law. I told them to send a policeman and an ambulance." He keyed the mike again. "And tell smoky to bring two pairs of handcuffs. We've caught ourselves two bad-boys."

"Will you be all right till they get here?" Jim asked Cal as he picked up his flashlight and rifle. "I'll go find Maddie." He trotted back to the shack and inspected the window where Maddie had escaped, then followed the path of broken weeds leading into the woods. "I wish I had my dog."

Jim moved into the woods, sweeping his flashlight back and forth over the ground and through the brush. Something red caught his eye. He stooped to pick it up. *A flower blossom? What's that doing out here in the woods?* He searched the ground around the spot. In the middle of the forest where humans seldom visited, was a footprint about the size of a woman's shoe. *Someone has been here, and not too long ago.* He continued to follow in the direction of the print hoping he was on Maddie's trail.

CHAPTER 25

Belva and Belinda prayed without stopping, knowing it was the only thing they could do to help find Maddie. Tires rolling on the gravels in the driveway sent them running to the window.

"It's the sheriff's cruiser," Belinda said, "but his blue lights aren't flashing. I hope that means they have good news."

Belva opened the door, her heart racing. "Did you find her, Sheriff Richards? Please tell me you found her!"

"Mrs. Randall, your husband is injured and we've called for an ambulance to take him to the hospital. He'll be okay. He took a bullet in his shoulder, but it's not life-threatening."

"Oh, no! How did he get shot? Where is Jim? And where is Maddie?" Belva sank into Cal's worn leatherette recliner. Belinda wrapped her arms around her momma's shoulders to console her, and the two of them cried together.

"Thanks to Jim and Cal, the two men responsible for her kidnapping are tied to a tree out on the Tolstory place. My deputy is out there now. Jim went out on his own to search for Maddie before we could get to the scene. The rescue squad is looking for him and Maddie. I'm sure we will find them soon, Mrs. Randall. In the meantime, why don't you and your daughter come with me? I'll take you to see your husband."

"Will you bring Maddie to us when you find her?"

"We will bring her to the hospital so she can be checked out as soon as we catch up to her."

***

"Stop! Stop the car!" Belinda bellowed from the backseat of the sheriff's cruiser. "That's Maddie! I saw her back there at that old barn road!"

Sheriff Richards slowed the car and came to a stop on the shoulder. "Are you sure you saw someone? It's not your wishful thinking playing tricks on you?"

"Yes, I'm positive. Turn around and go back! Hurry! I didn't imagine it. I'm telling you, I saw her!"

The sheriff backed his car as close to the ditch as he could without rolling into it and made a deep U-turn. When they approached the old barn road, he slowed to a crawl and switched his head lamps to high beam.

"Over there." Belinda pointed to a scrap of fabric clinging to a clump of blackberry briars. "That's where I saw her."

"I'll go check it out," the sheriff said as he moved the vehicle to the roadside. "You two stay in the car." Both of them got out of the car and followed him.

"Maddie!" Belinda called into the dark. "Where are you?"

Sheriff Richards turned to see Belva scampering toward the blackberry briars.

Maddie came running from behind the brush, arms wide and tears streaming down her cheeks, screaming, "Momma, Momma, Momma!"

"Well, I'll be—!" Sheriff Richards shook his head in amazement.

"Maddie, I've been so scared. Thank God, you are alive." Belva and Belinda held her and hugged her, kissing the tears off her face. "Are you all right? Did he hurt you? My sweet baby girl, your shirt is torn. What did they do to you?"

"I'm okay, Momma. My shirt caught on the briars when I ran into the bushes to hide. How did you find me?"

"Cal is hurt, Maddie. We were on our way to the hospital. He and Jim went out looking for you and they found the kidnappers. One of them shot Cal in the shoulder, but Sheriff Richards says he will be okay."

"Cal came looking for me? And he got shot chasing the kidnappers?" Maddie cried harder. "I thought he didn't love me, Momma."

The sheriff interrupted. "Cal and Jim both went looking for you, and Jim is still out there in the woods somewhere."

"No, he's not," a voice sounded from behind them. Everyone turned to see Jim hiking down the barn road with his rifle slung over his shoulder. He walked up to Maddie and handed her a red flower. "I think you lost this in the woods," he said.

Maddie hugged his neck, squeezing so hard he flinched. "Thank you, Jim. I'm glad you are a good hunter. I'll never complain again when you make us wait until you get back from hunting before we can eat Sunday dinner."

Jim swatted her backside with his hunting cap. "I'm holding you to that, little missy."

"Come on, folks," Sheriff Richards said. "Let's get Maddie to the hospital, then you can all go see Mr. Randall. This has been the strangest evening I've spent in twenty years. Kidnapping, drug dealers, citizens messing in police business, and a hippie in the briar patch. I need to write a book."

"Why *are* you dressed like a hippie, Maddie?" Belva asked.

"It's a long story, Momma. I'll catch you up on the way to the hospital."

"Well, young lady, I hope you have a good reason for being dressed that way. If I'd seen you out looking like that, I would have kidnapped you myself to get you off the street." Jim teased Maddie for her hippie attire. "My lands, girl! Where did you get that garb you're wearing?" He laughed and squeezed the breath out of her with his big bear hug.

CHAPTER 26

Two members of the rescue squad examined Dr. Mason and his thug. "I'd say these two have concussions, and Dr. Mason has a broken nose. We'll send a doctor to examine them when you get them locked up." The deputy removed Jim's ropes from his prisoners' wrists and secured their hands with cuffs.

"That man knows his knots," he said, as he struggled to untie Dr. Mason's hands.

"That man tried to kill me," Tolstory whined. "I want him arrested. He was trespassing on private property. He had no right to . . ."

"Shut up," the deputy said, "before I give you a matching lump on the other side of your head. You can tell it to your attorney if you can find one dumb enough to defend you." The deputy pushed Dr. Mason and Tolstory into the backseat of the cruiser and slammed the door.

The paramedics loaded Cal onto a gurney and rolled him toward the ambulance. Cal shivered when Zachariah's eyes met his in a death stare.

"I'll get you a blanket, Mr. Randall," the paramedic said before closing the ambulance door.

***

Two Weeks Later

Cal scanned the *Knoxville Journal* and told the news to Belva as they sipped their morning coffee. "The write-up in this morning's paper says the police raided East Side Medical Clinic and found boxes full of cocaine and heroin in a cabinet in Zachariah Mason's private office. And they found a notebook with names of reps from two major drug companies. They're checking out the drug suppliers and have arrested three of them. It doesn't look as if Mason will get away with it this time. That Tolstory fellow confessed to kidnapping Maddie. He said Dr. Mason ordered him to get rid of her for snooping around his clinic. He ratted him out good, even gave them the name of the drug runners on Mason's payroll. Frankie was one of them."

"I'm sorry Frankie died, but I am so thankful he didn't have time to involve Maddie in that drug scheme," Belva said. She topped off Cal's cup with the last of the coffee.

"Yeah, I doubt if she would have taken his drugs, but those pushers will do most anything to get people hooked so they can make their profit." Cal leaned back in his chair with his fingers laced together behind his head, a proud smile in his eyes. "I guess since Maddie can't be a boy, at least she's smart like her old man, huh?"

"Did you know Maddie thought you didn't love her? When she learned you had been shot while chasing her kidnappers, she realized that you do," Belva said.

His smile turned to a frustrated frown. "Girls expect men to be warm and fuzzy, spoutin' their feelings all over the place. A man shouldn't have to say what he feels."

"It wouldn't hurt to tell her once."

He tossed the dishtowel he'd used for a napkin onto his plate. "I have to get back to work this evening. I should make Maddie go back to work and help with the expenses around here. It was her foolishness that caused this mess."

Belva shook her head and rolled her eyes.

"What? How else will she learn to take responsibility for her actions? Women!" He shoved his chair back from the table. "I'm going in early today to make up for lost time."

***

"I wish Daddy would go to church with us," Maddie said to Belva when they met in the living room on Sunday morning. "Where is he anyway? I haven't seen him since breakfast."

"He's standing right behind you, young lady." Startled, Maddie jumped one step backward and tripped over his feet. "Don't mess up my Sunday shoes. You don't want to be ashamed of your old daddy, do you?"

She gawked at the military shine on his black wingtip slippers, his pale blue pin-striped dress shirt and charcoal gray slacks. "Are you going to church with us today? I can't believe it! Look at him, Momma. Isn't he handsome when he's dressed up?"

Cal backed away from them with a harsh frown on his face, and Maddie braced herself for an explosion. *I should have known. It will take more than a dress shirt and nice slacks to turn him into a gentleman.*

Moments passed without a word, then his frown melted to tears. "When I thought we had lost you. . ." He swallowed hard. "I thought about . . ., I don't know what I'd . . ." He raised his hands as if signaling a stop and cleared his throat. "I— love you, Maddie." His hands shook and his chin quivered.

"Daddy, I—"

Cal's face looked empty and desolate. He was so broken, yet she didn't have the courage, the want, or the ability to respond.

"I'm sorry, Daddy. But I can't— I mean, I don't know what to say."

"Just say you'll forgive me." He reached out, his arms open, inviting her into his embrace. "I'll be a better Daddy to you from here on out, or at least I'll try. I can't promise I won't mess up again."

The silence in the room swirled in Maddie's head. She stared at him, unable to believe that the man standing in front of her was Cal. In seventeen years, he had never once said he was wrong about anything, never apologized. He had never cried or shown any emotion other than anger or frustration. He had been ill-tempered, rude, and verbally abusive. Now he expected her to let it all go. She didn't know if she could. Would he be back to his old self again tomorrow, or the next day, or next week? How could anyone change that much so soon?

From a shadowy place inside her heart, Maddie heard Abba's gentle voice pleading with her. "I have loved you and forgiven you, Maddie. Love bears all things."

She turned to look at her momma. Belva nodded toward Cal and touched Maddie's elbow to urge her forward.

Her heart pounded and beads of sweat formed at the edge of her hairline. The Holy Spirit tugged and pulled at her conscience. Her breath came shallow puffs. She thought she might suffocate. She surrendered.

A touch from Abba sent a wellspring of humility and remorse surging through her prideful spirit, and the words came without effort.

"Okay, Daddy." She walked into his open arms and felt an unfamiliar and satisfying connectivity. "I'll try to do better too. Maybe we can all start all over together?"

"That's fair enough," he said. "But let's all start over in God's house and do it right this time."

He released her from his hug, held her at arm's length and explored her face. "I never noticed," he said. "You have my eyes."

About The Author

As a born again child of God, my greatest joy in life has been my family and sharing my spiritual experiences with anyone interested in hearing them. God has greatly blessed me with His continued love and protection and given me the greatest gift of all: a personal relationship with Him and the promise of eternal life.

My prayer is that this book will encourage you to seek His face, that you will accept His precious gift of salvation and allow Him to mold you into the best you that you can possibly be.

Other titles by Mary Ann Brantley
Acorns from Ivy – a novella
A true life story of overcoming bitterness, resentment, and hate by relying on God's promises and seeking his wisdom. The memoirs of a daughter born to a deeply-rooted Christian mother and a father with roots as shallow as trailing ivy.

Please visit my ministry website at https://acornsfromivy.wordpress.com and my author website at https://maryannbrantley.wordpress.com to subscribe to my blog
Like on Facebook   authormaryannbrantley

Twitter @brantleyma

God's Plan of Salvation

God is Holy—Man is not. Romans 3:23 For all have sinned and come short of the glory of God. Romans 3:10 As is it is written, "There is none righteous.

No, not one."

We must realize that we cannot have a relationship with God because sin separates us from Him. We must realize that we cannot save ourselves. Ephesians 2:8 For by grace are you saved through faith, and that not of yourselves. It is the gift of God.

God sent His Son Jesus to become a sinless sacrifice for all mankind that through Him we can be saved. (Romans 5:8 But God commends His love toward us, in that, while we were yet sinners, Christ died for us). John 3:16 For God so loved the world that He gave His only begotten son, that whosoever believes in him should not perish, but have eternal life.

Salvation is a free gift from God. God sent Jesus as the payment for our sin so that we may come to Him and have life. Romans 6:23 For the wages of sin is death; but the gift of God is eternal life through Jesus Christ our Lord.

We must believe that Jesus has paid that price for us and that He is our way to God. We must believe in our heart and confess that Jesus is Lord. Romans 10:9-10 That if you shall confess with your mouth the Lord Jesus, and shall believe in your heart that God has raised him from the dead, you shall be saved. For with the heart man believeth unto righteousness, and with the mouth confession is made unto salvation.

We must call upon his name, acknowledge and confess that we are sinners so that we may have the life He died to give us. Romans 10:13 For whosoever shall call upon the name of the Lord shall be saved.

Sinners' Prayer

Dear Lord,

I know I am a sinner and without you I am lost. I need your forgiveness. I believe that Jesus Christ died in my place and paid the penalty for my sins. I am now turning away from sin and I accept Jesus as my Savior. I commit myself to you. Please send your Holy Spirit into my heart to fill me and help me be the person you want me to be. Please save me Lord.

    Amen